W9-BZK-573

BO OK

by Ken Sparling

Pedlar Press | Toronto

ACKNOWLEDGEMENTS
The publisher wishes to thank the Canada Council for the Arts and the Ontario Arts Council for their generous support of our publishing program.

The author wishes to thank *New York Tyrant, No Colony,* and Mudlucious Press for their friendship and support.

LIBRARY AND ARCHIVES CANADA
CATALOGUING IN PUBLICATION

Sparling, Ken, 1959-
    Book / Ken Sparling.

ISBN 978-1-897141-33-5

    I. Title.

PS8587.P223B66 2010   C813'.54   C2009-907141-X

BOOK DESIGN Zab Design & Typography, Toronto
TYPEFACE Golden Cockerel

Printed in Canada

THE CANADA COUNCIL | LE CONSEIL DES ARTS
FOR THE ARTS | DU CANADA
SINCE 1957 | DEPUIS 1957

ONTARIO ARTS COUNCIL
CONSEIL DES ARTS DE L'ONTARIO

And what we break we may reshape, and that which fails might still succeed. We have found rich deposits of chance, and we will dig them out.

They had scarred, they had broken the world. And, in so doing, they set free forces that they were able to trap. Forces that allowed them to reshape things, to fail and succeed simultaneously because they mined for possibilities.

–China Miéville, *The Scar*

PART
1

1. Fog fingered up the steep slope from the river. It snaked through grass. Every push it made up the slope left it depleted. Only the breathiest whispers attained the ledge where the men slept. Sometime toward morning, the fog retreated. David never knew how close it had come to overtaking the camp. In the night, David dreamed of the girl in sunglasses, with long straight hair that fell like a sheet from the girl's scalp, but broke apart into ropes whose individual strands twisted together, but broke apart into wisps that curled gently at their ends, resolving into single, almost invisible strands, before settling around the girl's shoulders and breast bone. When David woke, the twin discs of the girl's sunglasses were burned into his memory. She had no eyes. She was like an insect. A red-faced man leaned over David. Pulled the sleeping bag away from David's face. David opened his eyes. They called this man Tan. But David had never seen him with a tan. He looked red. Always. Like he was on fire inside, although his calm features belied his fiery aura. His eyes were pale blue, almost colourless, deep and serene, like a pool

of water deep in a cavern where no wind disturbs the surface. Tan rarely smiled. But he was smiling now, his face a foot away from David's. He smelled of coffee and sleep. It wasn't quite morning. A thin scar of light breached the horizon, threatening to colour the sky the way a paint program splashes colour into a square set on a computer screen. In the faint light from the fire – someone must have built it up already – Tan's face actually looked tan. The man grinned fiercely in David's face, then stood suddenly, turned, bent to scoop some sticks from a pile of wood by the fire, and threw the sticks into the flames. Then Tan walked away. David stretched inside his sleeping bag.

Bicycles are such ridiculous creatures. Mom nodded. Bicycles are beautiful when you sit them in the sand on their kickstands. They never line up in perfect order. They aren't like an army, are they?

On a last note of interest, huxtable will not perish upon leaving the bed. Upon leaving the bed, huxtable simply ceases to be huxtable.

I want to remember everything. I want to start with the dead one. I want to remember how the dead one died. How the dead one died, along with the very fact of the dead one's dying. These are the hinge upon which my memories fold back and recover the dead one's life. The dead one's dying is the pivot from which I begin to remember my life.

Most people won't tell you the truth of what they hear when they hear you. They won't tell you they have heard your secret. They are afraid. If they can hear your secret, you might be able to hear theirs. So the real secret we go around trying to keep from each other every day is that we hear each other's secrets every day.

The road was empty, but for the stones that occasionally

sparkled in sunlight. The sun was alone in the sky. And the sun was hot. There would have been dust. The world whorled in dust. Dust would have risen most days, but today the air was utterly still. Insects drifted and swam in swarms like snow in wind. Peter looked sad. How far? he asked. Really far, she told him. Fuck.

Other people will hear your secret in everything you write. Most people will hear, not just the indecipherable hiss of a secret being whispered, but the actual meaning of your secret.

The beauty of conveying meaning in tone is the opening of the possibility of contradiction with the utterance of a single world.

Peter's eyes were shiny and crusted with goo. His nose was red and he pawed the ground with his foot like a restless animal.

This is a lie. I know this. If I remember his living before I remember his dying, it is only because I believe that no one will read of his living if they have already, in the words I write, found him dead. In each of the moments I remember, I configure his death. This is the nature of memory, the quality of memory that makes it so unlike life, so unlike living. Memory stomps on living in ways that make living seem thin. Like air in your hair. That quality of thinness a single strand of hair takes on when wind lifts it from a head and stretches it over the air.

A man went down to the lake to die. He was sad. His life had gone by fast. There was nothing left to do. He thought of reading a book, but he couldn't see the point. He wondered how he had ever seen the point. He thought about writing something. A poem, presumably. There wasn't time for anything else. But, when he got out his notepad and pen, he had no idea what to write. He had nothing left to say. He had the newspaper with him. He read the headlines. When he was done, he folded the paper and put it under a piece of driftwood to keep its pages from scattering across the beach in the wind.

God is one form of silence and discretion. His work once transcended the narrow boundaries of wordlessness by learning to make noises between the silent movements. Santa and God seem to live on and on. And Mary Poppins. She seems to live on and on, also.

He had never met a real writer. He decided to become one. He was a quiet, nervous boy, his teacher said, but he wrote sad stories. The new millennium seemed strange, and he began to grow obtuse. The depth and duration of his obtuse periods seemed to increase. You can only continue something till you die. His main project, at the time, seemed to be cutting out paper snowflakes. Had he never met a woman? This winter, it felt as though: no, he hadn't. Later, he met famous people. Pop journalists, and a photographer named Flag. His project now was to make a list of things he wanted to do before the end of August.

How do we open? The strength in openings, the delight of a new opening, the potential inherent in all openings, this is what leads us to open again and again. Seen in the light of the irresistible appeal of openings, not finishing isn't so much of a failing. It's more a gathering up, an embrace of the energy offered us in opening again today. The alternative is not to question the validity of your attachments, but to accept their momentary character and – is it possible? – to celebrate their transience. The modus operandi is never to question the validity of your accidents, but to regret the alternatives. You can open Friday like a ketchup bottle, but you still won't find what you're looking for.

Python's tomb in Greece is still there, tense between the hunger. Fill yourself with the hunger. Be hungry. You can still read the inscription. The hunger to move. Far enough away each day it has cast its shadow. According to the sun, the tension is where you live. Each single day presenting the opportunity for destruction.

The writing has to live statistically. It is astonishing. As a single icon, it stands for nothing but its own uncoiling.

Are we writing to see ourselves exposed, or externalized?

The car drove away. A tower of dust. You could see through the smoke swimming at the top of the hill. The sun went down. A cloud covered the moon. Paul turned. The car was gone. Someone else was in the car. Someone Paul didn't know. He tried to fix the colour of the car in his head. Blue, he said. Blue.

Hair was on the floor. Many hairs were staying together in groups. Some single hairs floated, but finally got on the floor and other hairs joined them. No one hair could stay on its own once it hit the floor.

2. Cash transactions took place while the girl's hair fell gently to the floor. He held onto his wallet. He passed money to the girl. He looked directly in her eyes. The girl took his money. She looked blue. Her eyes were young. Her hair looped. Behind her eyes, she smiled. She must work here part-time, he thought.

Paul was a tree. He was ahead of his time. He was beside where he was. Then he was behind where he was. But Mike is a poetry. Mike rhymes when he's with me. Much like a poetry, at his best, Mike causes groups of words to congregate. You can't lie on a poem, Mike, the way you can lie on a bed.

What we do, each of us, in the literature of our existence – what we write in our diaries at night, what we choose to add to our meals, what we wear when we sit in front of the TV in a dark room in the middle of winter – some might call this a way of acting. I wrote a stupid letter this morning. I wrote it as though it were something other than what it is. As though I know the date, the time, the location. It is clear that I wrote the correct date at the top of the letter. Out of my utter confusion about everything, I had envisioned what was probably the most abstruse system of getting organized anyone could possibly concoct. Within two weeks of implementing my new system, my life had gone from a disorganized shambles to a chaotic nightmare almost hallucinogenic in nature. When I got home, I parked the car. Spending the day with my son and his class at the outdoor recreation centre at that school you used to go to had been a mistake. A school not in your area is not a mistake. But this trip in the car was a long wander over turf with no proper boundary. Go. Have lots of fun. Watch your progeny laugh. Your belonging depends upon your skill at keeping the program in hand. On the other hand, the balcony is negligible. The stretch of your chin is negligible. Even the ear on rows of air is negligible. Think the crack of your mouth. Feel the petty convenience.

But what day will it be when you turn the page of your book? You will never turn the page of your book. You must realize you are lost. You can try to find your way back. You can move forward. You can count your losses. You can further your losses. But there is nothing further from loss than the particular losses you count as only your own.

I got two letters. One was from Brad and it said that Peter is tall, but that his long hair is very straight, and his worldly languidness is very graceful, even equine at times. The other letter was from Roger and it said that he felt synchronous to that place where he seemed uncomfortable with the distance he felt himself from the ground.

I don't myself send letters. Every once in a while, I get a letter. I don't know why.

I need to go home, but I'll try again another time.

The girl got off her white coat. The girl with no hat got off her shoes. In the end, the girl in the black cap was all that was left. But then another girl in a black cap turned up. Like a miracle. Together, these two hatted girls were quiet, whispering their hunger like stallions breathing steam in cold air. They stood by one of the poles in the centre of the aisle, their peaked caps nearly touching. They viewed the world, but only out the corners of their eyes. Collectively, they had four eyes. All four of the girls' eyes slid slowly about in their eye sockets, while the heads of the two girls stayed still. When their stop came, the girls got off with their hands in their pockets. There were other girls, too. Older girls. Girls with briefcases on wheels. Girls in coats of black leather, their wistfully straight hair lying dormant. But they travelled no more than a stop or two. When they rolled off the train, their hair rose slightly, as though electric, rippling with currents of invisible gold spark.

We're here! Mary! Look up! Mary looked up. They were, indeed, here.

They sit on the visitor chair, but they aren't even visitors. I put them there, like slaves. Visitors can leave when they want. In my workspace, the people who come to see me can't sit down. They look awfully scared. I keep telling myself I should just return them. All this shit makes people so scared. Can I sit down when they come to see me? It's utterly hopeless. I want to write things that disappear as soon as they get read, or that aren't even there in the first place. How do you write that? But I also want the nearness of redemption the way I want the warmth of the sun some days. That feeling of being like sand on a beach with no reason to exist. Just an accident of pummelling. Leaving you ugly and forgotten. Forgotten and free. I believe this to be the substance of redemption. Don't hold the day tight, as though it were a cold thing and not a corner of the room.

The silver angels fell, sizzling on the atmosphere. They had screamed and then they had broken away. There was something in what I said that they didn't want to hear. When I said it, it became a matter of pride.

I started reading your book a while back. I did not continue. Lately I've been completely overwhelmed. The last thing that gave me any sense of buoyancy was the moon. Before that, it was a girl in a breeze. Before that it was some strains of music from some bands in subway stops I visited. Once, long ago, it was something I saw by a river.

I just finished getting kicked in the gut. But I don't mean it that way. I don't mean to hurt anyone with these things I say. I know no one kicked me in the gut for real. I know what's real. I just wanted to tell you what I appreciate. You know enough to want to make the effort. But you haven't got the energy right now.

We went to a wedding yesterday, or so we thought. Today, we are pretty out of it. The thing that is central to all of this is the idea of a wedding. Here is an emotional matrix at work. It spreads all over the world. Because of the uselessness that precludes all who came to the wedding, it was a day of fun. It was the wedding of my cousin to a guy she was already married to. They were married in Australia the first time. My cousin was doing post-doctoral work in microbiology. The priest at the second wedding said, A person can know all about the mysteries of life – like the mysteries of microbiology – but, without love, it means nothing. After they got married the first time, my cousin and this guy spent a bit of time together in Australia. Then my cousin's husband had to come back to the United States.

Her body resonates like something cut through with sharp steel and it has blown her to the far edge of sorrow. Speaking of meaning, though, there are squeaks of meaning. Some squiggles. Some dark forms. Some letters below. I can see!

The damp man still has eyes. The damp man's eyes are still open. The damp man's eyes are unblinking in horror. Presumably, the door behind the damp man led to the kitchen.

They left blinking at Litre's husband. Litre's husband still damp from his fall into the river. On the stone steps of the castle, men sit and watch the sky above. A hawk man with wax wings circles, looking for something to eat. A bird of prey cries out. The hawk man circles beneath dark clouds that roll like tire tracks across a sky full of wind. Two men who had thought Litre's husband a goner took him away from the dump. The two men looked up when they heard the bird man's wings beating against the wind. It's an omen, said the shorter man. The other man, tall and rangy, holding the handles of the barrow they'd hauled the damp man to the castle in, regarded his short companion. They both looked back at the damp man.

3. A space opens among words. Move the words apart. Wire the sentences to the page. Lean over the spaces you've made. Do you think they will all be the same? It must be part of the problem that won't go away. Make the sentences cold and unknowable. Every single sentence you've written, let this happen. They won't fight back. Sentences don't fight back. They get empty. Fake. They get hard. At some point the words will change. Twist. The words seem to open very wide. When the sentences seem to point and grin at you, indifferent, grab the paper. Watch the words appear beneath your hands. Run your hands over the paper.

I stayed up half the night crying. I was copying diskettes onto other diskettes. And then: I was copying everything onto the hard drive. In the morning the sun looked like a replica of the real sun I'd seen from time to time in movies.

The wind must have been a corporeal thing. Cooperating, Mary was afraid the wind would get to be more than it already was. It would get in the food. Ruin it. The man went into the yard. He smoked. He talked to Mary through the kitchen window. It made Mary happy, later, to find someone sitting in her living room with his boots on the coffee table. There are no bus stops along the stretch of road where Mary is parked tonight. Mary is parked in one of the parking lots on the far side of the university. Her shoes look angry. Red pants. Blue-green elevator shoes. Stanchions vibrate around her like water in a glass on a kitchen table. Her hat is black. Her heart torn. A face comes out of the blackness. She wakes. Goes down to the kitchen. The stairs creak. The house hums. Soothing. The timbers creak. As though someone has entered the house. Was there light in the kitchen? The hall was dark. The kitchen had a swinging door. It might be sunshine. The door swung. Sun flooded the kitchen. The sink shone. Beneath the sill, a small china pot held a small green plant. Beside it, a ripe tomato tilted slightly. Mary's housecoat: bright yellow, a cone of light falling from her neck, encircling her feet. Her eyes tired, but relaxed. Her face white. Her eyebrows serious.

The hairless one chuckled. Having a friend forced him to look around. See a little. He saw all around him on the bus. The spike-haired one laughed bitterly. They rode the bus together. It was early morning. They practically never had any place to go. As they grew older, their pain would lessen.

The many girls stopped moving. They had been moving along together. The white girl hopped from one foot to the other. Mary didn't hear what they were saying. They were fourteen years old, Mary believed. Or fifteen. They were full of something they'd never been seen with before. Three of the girls moved together as a unit. One of the girls backed away. The other girls advanced on her. One girl wore her black baseball cap like a weather front receding off a continent. Her eyes flashed like lightning. Her body whistled like wind. They got to the end of the platform. The back-up girl backed up against the wall. The advancing girls stood close. They laughed like rain running up a stairway. I'm only what they want me to be on Fridays, Mary realized, when I'm too tired to be anything else, when the weekend looms like the small song of a little girl alone on a beach after her parents swim out to the horizon and five days later they have not come back. The police will come, sure, but the girl's small song will remain the same through all the days of her life. You will never know what day it is. Mary lay in the heat. Steam rose around her face. The water covered her up to her neck. The ends of her black hair swam around her face, freed briefly from gravity. Never fear falling, she whispered. I need a new base of operations, such as the place under the trees we used to go to when we were children. It was on the side of that little hill that looked like an embankment by a river, and, in fact, might once have been an embankment for a river, if it was wider, but now it was the year 2070. About two hundred feet away, across a field that looked suspiciously like a flood plain, or even an old riverbed, especially in the imagination of a seven-year-old boy and his six-year-old sister.

There was a spot open near the entrance, so the old man eased his car in. He eased his old body out of the car. There was a thin rain falling, icing the pavement. If it were a little colder out, the rain would be snow, thought the old man. And if it were a little warmer out, all this ice would be puddles. The old man eased his feet slowly over the ice, keeping his hand on the car to balance himself. So treacherous, he thought, and he felt the sound of this lovely, thick, substantial word tremble tenuously as it entered his thoughts, like something coming apart in soup. So he spoke the word aloud, whispered it really: treacherous.

reformatted in terror and everything new is terrifying, too. I lean my forehead against the steering wheel and try to figure out what's gone on in the last twelve years. Maybe it's too late. Maybe there's nothing I can do to turn this thing around.

Lightning bolt gift wrap was the item to remember. I couldn't remember it. I couldn't remember where I'd put the lightning bolt gift wrap. I couldn't remember where I'd put the gift I was going to wrap in the lightning bolt gift wrap, either. Furthermore, I couldn't remember where I'd decided to store any of the gift wrap. There were other sheets of gift wrap. It wasn't all lightning bolt gift wrap. Some of the gift wrap had dogs on it. Some had words. Some had baseball mitts. Some had Model T cars. I used to keep the gift wrap in the top desk drawer, but it wasn't there anymore. I couldn't remember where I'd put the gift wrap. There were other things I couldn't remember, too.

I went back to sleep. Back to the dream. But not the one about Junior Miller. Finally, a new one. I felt better when I got up. My back hurt, but not as bad as the day before. I peeled the potatoes with the window open, listening to the birds, but also singing my own song. A song of love.

Those days are over, he said. They were listening to his live CD. Do you miss those days, I asked. Naw. Those days are gone. I love what I'm doing now. What *are* you doing now? I asked. I don't really know, he said.

"I can't abide the fracturing of the present by the intrusion of a planned future. Probably I just don't want to die."
—Jenny Diski, *On Trying to Keep Still*.

4. He passes five black girls. They might be sisters. One of them might be the mother. Elderly people walk toward Major Mackenzie. There are no other people on the street. Just cars. Ramming things. Trees. Someone hits a bus shelter. People are running up and down Yonge Street. Swimmers camp by the road like dead animals made of silicon. He sits against the wall. Legs tucked up against his chest. Knees poking through the ring his arms make. He is, once again, only whatever he was before. He walks like a whisper. Think again of supper. Pass a woman in wind, hair floating like a parachute. In front of a store, a man is cleaning the window. He spreads soap. He scrapes soap away. He squeegees soap off. Once he is finished, he steps back. Looks at the window.

I had the worst possible sleep last night. I kept waking up. I was afraid. I figured if I stayed awake I would be okay. I was sweating like a pig. I couldn't open the window. I knew the birds would be out soon. They sit in the trees outside the window. Call to each other. Call to me.

Stop in at the video store on the way home. There will be about fifty people in there. Down the block from the video store, you can buy bagels. He walks around. Talks to himself in French. Feels foolish. He knows he's not going to rent a video. Everyone in the store aimless. They've come to be with other people. Not to get videos. Only now they've got here and there are people all around them and all they can think to do is mill around. She sits in the lee of a building. A tall building. Back on the side streets, he passes walking dogs. Older ladies sit together in the shadows at the backs of stores. Books give off a dusty heat. They draw the moisture out of people's eyes. At the first display, a woman stops. Picks up a book: *How to Save Texas*.

The cab pulled into the terminal. Grace remained calm. She reclaimed her hand. The driver set the suitcase on the curb. Arthur waited. He knew if he waited long enough, something would happen. The cab drove through the intersection. Disappeared. Red tail lights lost among other red tail lights. Rain fell on Grace's things.

What is at stake? Conjoney's emptiness invades the boy. The boy feels suddenly strong. With a depth of clarity he has never experienced, the boy stares into the fiery veil of smoke and there conjures the story of the mist within the smoke. Conjoney feels like a tree smashed out of the way for a new road.

I took her skating once. She could skate pretty good. We had a good time. She kept laughing. I don't think she was listening to anything I said. It was winter. It was so cold. When I looked up to start the car to drive her home, there was steam all over the windows.

Clementine was forever thinking up ways to make more money. To pay her parents. To get her jewellery back. When she wasn't coming up with ways to make money, she made curtains. She cleaned the mirrors in the bathrooms. Ate grapefruit. Turned off every light in the house. She sat in the glow of the streetlight that was outside the apartment coming in the window. She looked like a ghost.

5. There was something incursive in the skin of the apple, which sat on the car seat abandoned like the crust of something at the edge of a place no one ever goes in a world we can't imagine during a time in the distant future when silver planets rip natural laws all to fuck.

I need your keys, Grace said. Leave your keys in the apartment when you go. Arthur felt he was falling apart. He felt he was a part of all things. Grace turned to look at him. She took his hand. Arthur let her. He let her hold his hand. He let her run her fingers over the back of his hand. He didn't look at her. He didn't look at anything.

Listening to God, he had found that he now wanted to go into the building. He stepped forward. He had so missed the boat. He only noticed Miriam when she went wild each day after lunch, throwing her acid brown hair around like a death metal kid. He did only what he noticed needed doing. Maimed, out on the pavement, he saw his foot get rolled over again. Spinning and flipping in circles, apparently wounded to the point where he could no longer hope to move freely. He went inside. Turned on the photocopiers.

They heard about the garden on the radio. Stories of its infinite healing power, its capacity to calm the frenzied soul, its beauty and savagery, its connection to beginnings. The stories they heard captured the imagination. But these stories were, necessarily, a gloss. They captured the surface of the garden. But not the part that was buried in the muck. The sharp teeth and bloody torn flesh.

The next morning, Tommy woke. My dad's an idiot, he thought. I'm the son of an idiot. He hung his legs over the edge of the bed. When they came, they came to places no one would have suspected. They were all downstairs in one room. The rest of the house was too hot. They were the only house in the neighbourhood that didn't have air conditioning. If he bent his hand over and squeezed it a certain way, it looked gnarled and arthritic. The house smelled like hot dogs. There were small places. Out-of-the-way places. Nothing much ever happened in these places. Everything happened.

She kept pulling the sheet over the boy, but the boy kept kicking it off again. The woman is hard to live with in the summer. She says things she wouldn't normally say. Fuck. Or shit. She turns her back on the sun. Good night, she says. The man sleeps. He tries to get the sleep to go out the edge of the blankets, but somehow it gets trapped in a pocket under the blankets and captures his eyes like slaves. One day, the heater comes on.

Everything screams spring. I get home. I want my life back, I tell the woman. In the cupboard, under the kitchen sink, there are things I haven't seen for years. Flowers are blossoming in the front garden. In his mind, he is walking down a staircase.

Five years ago, he planted a tree. He moves up the stone path.
Stands at the front door.

This is what I was doing. I was bringing my coffee out to the car in the morning. The sun burned my neck. It was only April and the air was cold. But it was after lunch and the sun burned the back of my neck. The breeze skittered low. Sand arrived from the south. You couldn't see the south end of the beach. It went on till it turned. The sky hung low over the horizon. But here, above us, it rose like an example of things we'd not imagined quite yet. It was the mother of all ceilings, that sky. For it looked like the blue end of up. To the north, past the plastic likeness of the mallard duck a cottager had settled over a rock cairn twenty feet from shore, you could see the nuclear power station.

He thought if he waited long enough, the little campers would calm down and stop talking amongst themselves. He thought he could just keep waiting and that eventually one of them would tell him what this was all about. The ogre had an eye where his belly button should have been. Even more disgusting, he had two belly buttons where his eyes should have been.

6. Have you seen this? Dickie asked. What is it? I said. A map of my route, Dickie said. Dickie put his cigarette to his lips. Sucked. I'm supposed to drive around this loop. Dickie waved the hand with the cigarette, painting a picture with smoke. Smoke looped around Dickie's face, wreathed Dickie's head. A blue cloud. I'm supposed to pick up any kids I see. Dickie held the map in my face. Then, Dickie said, but he hesitated, wiggled his cigarette like he couldn't get the words out. I could almost see Dickie's eyes through the smoke. If I don't think I've got the bus full enough, Dickie finally said, I'm supposed to go around the loop again and get more kids. Dickie dropped his arm and the map fell away. He put the cigarette to his lips. Looked out the window.

In the story that is about to unfold, four men see mountains. The mountains are still far off. The men are far off, too. They are on the far side of a distance they cannot abide. On the far side of the great plain, they see the mountains. Above the mountains, they see steamy black smudges of smoke-like cloud clawing toward them on prevailing winds. They see, directly above them, sky that is perfect in its attempt at being blue. All but one of the men, in their green uniforms and mirror sunglasses, feel themselves smile. They like to smile, huddled around the jeep that will take them to their deaths.

He came from a family. Not Mormons, exactly. Not aphrodites. Not phantasms. Nor crooks. Not pilots. Not cooks. Not any of these. For a while, he felt as though there was nothing he could think that someone else couldn't think better.

As the story went, a man of great gusto was about to fold his laundry. A woman came in. When she opened the door, a gust of wind sucked the man's socks and underwear out into the street. The socks and underwear landed in a puddle by the curb. The man of great gusto and the woman who had just come in stood at the window of the laundromat together and watched a truck drive over the man's underwear and socks. The wedding is in three weeks, the woman said, shadows of the letters of the word laundromat etched on her face where they carved their presence in glass before her. You should be able to fit into your suit by then. He looked up at her. Stood her up on her skates. Nobody had expected this much progress. For a while there, whenever he got home from work, the woman was standing outside. She was on the bottom step of the front porch. The light over the door had burnt out a couple of weeks ago. The man of great gusto had replaced the burnt out bulb with a fresh, crystalline hundred-watt bulb. Now, as he came down the road from the bus stop, he could see the woman standing in that light from the new hundred-watt bulb. There were marshes far to the north where men stumbled, their faces in a half-inch of water, drowning them.

When God destroyed his manuscript, he did it because he

felt he'd failed to achieve what he'd set out to do. He tried, as always, to help his sister-in-law. He tried to help her whenever he could. He felt privileged to have a sister-in-law. Having a sister-in-law made him special. I'm a special God, he thought. He called up his sister-in-law. Hi, he said. It's God. Hi, the sister-in-law said. It's me, he said, God. Hi, the sister-in-law said. The sister-in-law sounded disappointed. The sister-in-law lived in Edmonton. God called her at eight-thirty in the evening. The sister-in-law had been in Edmonton for four months. She'd been in Edmonton ever since she got married. She didn't have a job. She had a cat. She sent God videotapes where the cat was lying on the kitchen counter. In the videotape, the sister-in-law was making pasta salad. The cat was asleep on the counter beside the pasta salad. In the videotape, the sister-in-law talked to the cat. She mixed things into the pasta salad. She whistled. She sang. She told the cat a story.

All had heard stories about the place they were going. All had discounted those stories. Myths, they said. Fairy tales. But the man who didn't smile did not discount the stories. He already lived in a world far funkier than anything in any of those fucking fairy stories they were always telling.

The woman pulled her shirt apart, ripping the buttons. She started putting all the bed things over on her side of the bed. She threw Puffly, the pink stuffed thing she'd had since she was little, at the man's face. She was singing Over the Rainbow. She said, I hate this pillow. She threw it. It hit the man's head. Christ, the man said. The woman pulled on the bed things more. Any other rotten things you want to say to me? she said. Nothing I can think of, the man said. He was trying to remember something. Coming home from the bus stop after work. He'd cut through the ravine. His feet sank into snow. He was about to look at his watch. But he emerged from the ravine in the nick of time. He was in the schoolyard. He saw the neighbour's dog. The light was failing. The sun gone down behind the trees and houses that stretched forever in every direction. The neighbour's dog was coming down from the top of a snowbank. Then the neighbour herself came down the snowbank. Her coat was open. Her face red from wind. Her blackened hair flying free around her red face. For a while there, I felt like I was king of the castle, the neighbour said. She sat in the snowbank. Got out her notebook. Started writing something.

One of the dogs, a Doberman, was large. The other, very small. The small dog was some kind of mutt. The two dogs crossed each other's paths. The woman was trying to keep their leashes from crossing. You fuckers, she said. She wrenched the small dog back. It squeaked. The big dog trotted along, its tongue dripping.

We are all cows, the woman says. We are all cows, the boy repeats. We are the cows, the woman says. The cows are in the barn, the boy says. Are we in the barn? the woman says. The cows don't like the cold, the boy says. When will we come out? the woman says. Summer, the boy says. Who is in the barn with us? the woman says. Horses, the boy says. This is when the man says something. The man is driving.

7. There aren't many people. A man is raking leaves. Four houses away, another man is raking leaves. There are many leaves. Leaves rest on lawns. Leaves sit crooked. Leaves teeter on lawn ornaments. Leaves drown in bird baths. Bits of breeze cause leaves to hop. Leaves are crushed onto streets. Some leaves are just dark stains now on the sidewalk. Like memories of leaves. Leaves drift down out of high trees. Big, brown, threatening leaves. The wind rises. The wind rips. Leaves are ripped all to fuck. It rains leaves. Everything wet. Fecund. The sun refracts. Drops of water poised on leaf tips. A woman stands on her front porch in a housedress. The woman holds a steaming mug of coffee out in front of her. An offering. A car drives by. A teenager skates past on rollerblades. A woman runs. There are dogs behind her.

Listening to a good story, you go to sleep. Obliterate the horrible shape of the world. Impeding the shape of the tale, I followed an angel once. I saw the angel leave the building where I work. The angel turned right. Crossed at the crosswalk.

A man was crossing the other way. He didn't see the angel. Only I could see the angel. The building behind us tossed a certain light across the street. The building housed a public swimming pool. Across the road from the pool was the cemetery. The angel entered the cemetery. The main gates opened. The angel walked in like she was on her lunch hour. The grass next to the road was wet. Halfway to the greenhouse, the angel turned. Her shoes of a silver corbonite. She stood among gravestones. Followed a row of stones. She arrived at a bench. Sat. She stared up. The sky packing clouds. At a distance, which was absolute, the spotless blue directed the range and focus of the angel's regard.

His wife tried again and again, but failed. God left the room. Some fragments of nothing drifted up. The fireplace flue was open. Up the flue were stories about God. About people associated with God. Although I have gotten down on my knees to look up into the chimney, I have made no effort to assemble the reminiscences and fragments I've seen in the fireplace flue. They come to us as drifting smoke. They rise like smoke out of a chimney, then drift, disperse and get their smoky smell in your hair and clothes.

I'll go out now, she thought, but she didn't move. Whatever had stirred her to leave her bed, to come out here to the front room, stayed her now. Her legs felt heavy. Floorboards creaked. Her father parted curtains. Tweezered blinds. He stood in the front room on the threshold of her room. He didn't come in. He looked in. She swam two lengths of her mind. Stopped. Hung her arm over a lane rope. Pulled her goggles off. Fiddled with the strap. Her father waited, a handful of curtain clutched in his palm. She swam two more lengths. Stopped. Hung her left arm over a lane rope. Pulled her goggles overtop her head. Held them out. Examined the strap. Adjusted it. Pulled the goggles over her head. Did six lengths. Stopped. Hung on the wall. Pushed up over the edge of her mind. Crossed the deck, dripping. The bench where her t-shirt lay with her shorts was around the other side of her mind. She grabbed her gear. The goggles were good now. She was very skinny. She looked to her father, still holding the curtain, still in his bathrobe.

We were left behind to learn a language. Any language. Around us, jungle rose. In my mind I stayed aboard the ship. For many days nothing happened. By the time Pizarro returned with a new and bigger ship, I was part of the jungle and my Spanish brothers seemed strange.

They both looked up. Their faces raised to the light. Shallow pools of hope projected skyward. They were like angels. A handful of seagulls sculled across the sky. Scratched at the grey wall of cloud hanging over their hovering bodies. Land as far as the eye could see. The boy felt a kinship with the gulls. Not as one among them. As though he was all of them at once. His soul splashed the sky. Drops of paint dabbled onto white paper. The rain stopped. The sky stood dark. The wind gusted. Tossed water out of trees. Splattered puddles. Hit God and his wife on the head. As if they were Adam and Eve under trees in the garden. It wasn't ever going to be perfect, God thought, holding the umbrella over his wife's head. You might have thought his wife dead. She stood like a statue, not acknowledging her husband's words. They looked to the sky. He held her hand. It's these trees, oddly angled against wind, that stand past accountability. It's this feeling of wind. It touches you. This wind gives meaning. Something to take away. But this wind also takes something away as it skirts about you. It takes away what we fail to heed.

Two young girls, possibly Roman girls, one on rollerblades, one on a bike, searching for another language, a language of falling bodies and blood, stop talking when they see me coming. I stop where the river goes under the road. Look over the railing. The water looks cold. There is one of those giant-sized white plastic margarine buckets sitting upside-down in the water. Two fat people get out of a minivan in a driveway across the road. They have groceries. The first night I stayed over at Harold's place, he told me we'd be sleeping in the same bed. This ain't the Taj Mahal, he said. Just don't touch me. It was a small bed. I had trouble not touching him. I got very little sleep.

In this lifetime, if we are to believe reports and references we read in major publications, we must understand what we encounter each day as a metaphor for living. If God himself were to publish a number of works of literature and speculation, would we believe that what we are about to read presents life, not only in content, but in form? In the place we find within our lives one day, do we harbour hope, like God, that we will eventually complete a manuscript worthy of the fire?

I was reading a book. I heard the silence. Like falling. I went to the window. Looked out. The units across the street. The rain in the trees. I opened the window. Someone's car door slammed. I tried to see. Who was it? I went downstairs. Stood in the kitchen. The boys were asleep. I love the silence of snow falling outside the big front window. Big flakes drifting. The sound implicit in bigness; the silent betrayal of that implication through plate glass. The humming of the candy and coke machines in the front lobby. The silence of the furnace kicking in. The whispery silence of hot air through a vent in the floor.

The farmer knows that every cent he earns is beyond the cent he earned the moment before. The event of not knowing is not spurious. A species of fir is a tree only in a manner of speaking. A manner of blurring. The world, a blur of trees, turns

8. David looked at Mary. If you have to take a feeling, Mary, he said, take hope. He seemed to be considering what should come next. If I had taken all my feelings and held onto them, he whispered, while simultaneously abandoning hope, I would never see the falling sky again, or feel the things I longed to feel. He moved his head. Slowly, he looked around the children's area. What are we? he thought. We are what we never could have been? What could we have been? he asked. We could have been what we never could have been. What they could have been was what they never were. He felt as though he'd woken up to find himself someplace he hadn't known about. He felt like he'd found himself someplace where he was happy. David looked back at Mary. She could see in his eyes his testimony. His testimony was unspoken. His hesitation gone. He'd reached a decision. Each step I take forward, David told her, moves me further away from the place I am trying to go. The place I am trying to go is a place I've been, although I couldn't tell you exactly where it is. I couldn't tell you when I first was there. To

go there I do not have to leave here. I am, at times, permitted to visit this place again, but not when I want to, nor when I feel the need. Stand ahead of all you signify, David said. Exist previous to all you prevent. Bring what you hear into existence. In this way, walk out into a sun and be the deep rags of grey cloud you see above you.

At night, the man turned into a butterfly. David paused. Mary understood that he wasn't trying to decide anymore. He seemed to be navigating Mary. Measuring her response. Twisting the telling. Waiting to see if she could take it. What does he want? Mary thought. She wanted him to carry on with the story. She wanted to hear the soft timbre of his voice. To see the softening of his face as he lost himself in the account.

Louella got into this parking lot patrol thing when the weather turned nice. There was a blue van with a flat tire that never moved. There was a Cadillac that was there in the corner, under the big pine tree. It was very blue. Louella sat in the sunshine. Her flared shorts flaring. Her clipboard in her lap. Beyond the parking lot was another parking lot. Louella sat with her mirrored sunglasses, her furious, unquenchable rage making her breath come ragged. Pale numbers flashed before her eyes. Descriptions of cars. Cars she had never seen. Cars she had never ridden in as a child. Cars she had never yet even seen on TV. A large, dilapidated apartment complex sat like a series of ruins down the road and across the street.

Mary was afraid. If she did the wrong thing, David would certainly cease to tell his story. It's as if he's checking to see if I have the stomach for it, she thought. The stomach for what? she thought. The truth, she realized. She relaxed. She hadn't known it, but David had been on the verge of ending his story. He'd been watching Mary twist. Mary had been watching her hands. Now she saw her hands relax. She looked into David's eyes. He gazed back. He must have seen what he wanted to see. He took up the story again. He didn't stop now until most of an hour had past. He stood. I have to pee, he said. For a moment, David travelled to the bathroom in the story, lost to Mary. Mary lost to herself. Mary walked David to the back door. She offered to walk him home. But her offer seemed fragile. It collapsed in the silence of the glow the boy broadcast under the light above the back door. Mary stepped out the door. They moved through the back alley into the street. She watched the boy walk into darkness, resurfacing now in the pool of light from a street lamp. Disappearing into dark. Again resurfacing. When she could see him no longer, she went back into the library to gather her things. She went to the children's area. Her bag sat on the floor by the chair, along with the book and the remains of her lunch. She sat down in the story room chair. The child does not want to kill the father, she dreamed. The child loses interest. He comes to God by another path. When he's too tired to kill the father, he looks for something to read. A magazine. A book about fathers. Not the earthly fathers we all know from childhood. Not the creator we know from the Bible. Rather, the one we get from *Nintendo Power*. A father looks into space. In the air between cars in the parking lot, where a boy will not follow, he steps through the space and does not look back.

You've got to fold the flag a certain way, the old man said. There's only one right way to do it. He held the corners of the flag high up, keeping the bottom of the flag well off the ground. First, get it like this, he told the boy. Hold it here. And here. Keep it off the ground. If it touches the ground, you have to burn it. Do you understand? If it touches the ground, it's ruined. It's no good to anyone anymore. Like this. Like this. Like this. Got it?

The old man handed the folded flag to the boy. Unfurl it. The boy unfurled it. A corner of the flag fell away, caught wind, dipped, rose, settled on the ground. The old man looked at the place where the flag was touching the ground. We'll have to burn it, he said. He looked away. Touched his face beneath his eye. Turned. Went and left the boy standing with the flag in the front yard with no sounds anywhere except a very faint bit of wind catching in the trees and, very far off, the sound of a transport truck on the highway near Beaverton.

I felt a fear developing directly through the process of getting ready. The feeling I felt, the feeling – I'll call it fear – the feeling of fear I felt was ripe. Translation was imminent. Translation takes faith. Faith is the translator. The more deeply and vitally you live your life, the more afraid of dying you will become. Ironically, tragically, frighteningly, but absolutely understandably, you are tempted to remain far below sea level. To protect yourself. You are simply protecting yourself. From death.

The story the boy had been telling had left Mary feeling sad, but at the same time, at least for as long as David was telling the story, she had felt exhilaration. Like a new possibility had suddenly presented itself.

You may convince yourself that you aren't living in the area you had once hoped to live. A place surrounded, tucked in, embellished, lapped upon. Your fullest potential becomes your deepest dearth. A lack of resources is a lack of time. And a lack of time is a lack of money. Lack of friends is whatever it is – but...what is a life without the lies? And what a lie it is. Because the prospect of living your wilful existence – re the potential you garner at every moment of your life – your full potential is the name of God. And God, full potential takes a lot of energy. Every fucking limitation of time, money, friends and whatever

else is afflicting you – afflicting your body, afflicting your soul,
afflicting your eyes and your hair and your humour, afflicting
all of you with venomous fury – today, your full potential is
exactly the extent of your willingness to be and be done with
whatever is at hand.

I was twelve. The floor began to shake. We went to the edge
and looked over. Several times I felt at a loss. I was only the wind,
I told him. That bastard.

9. I saw a creature with a tail but no head. I saw winged creatures that may or may not have been birds. I saw a woman with a ponytail and a beard. I saw a ragged shoreline. A tree with a horse's head. The shoreline transformed into a dwarf. A kangaroo with a baby in her pouch. The magic table was as beautiful as ever. With its delicious, beautiful, ridiculous, impossible, wonderful stories – stories he starred in. It was already around midnight. It was dark. I don't know what I was doing. I might have been cooking something smooth. I moved to the other side of the table. The terrible images disappeared. The images were random green splotches, and for a time they remained like that. I played a game of solitaire. I won. I looked down at the table. Under the cards, scattered, I saw a fox on its hind legs, head thrown back in a dance.

After I'd written that first sentence, I became more methodical. That's been facilitated by two Germans, Jorg and Ferdinand. They write because of that kid. I met them at a bar. Germans, they told me, are more knowledgeable than the

Dutch. I was talking drunkenly about the idea of writing and they told me they'd written something once in Köln. That's why they moved here to Holland, supposedly. They seemed really calm about things. When I was sure they were cool, I just casually mentioned the two sentences I had written. They seemed amazed. Someone recently read one of my books, Jorg said.

Clouds fall apart at the top of mountains. Forests flush forth. Huge green arrows carved into trees. Palaces rise up. It's coming, he says. There is rain on the front windshield. It has been coming for thirty-eight years. What are the places in this world that are all in shadow? he wondered. When those places are very large, he told himself, they can sometimes seem quite frightening. But, at the same time, they are quite exciting. Out in the open, he murmured, where the sun shines, you can see things approaching from a great distance. This gives you time to figure out what they are and who they belong to. You can gauge intentions. But in shadow, things come upon you very quickly. It can be difficult to know what you are seeing.

Gertrude was her name. You're one of the chosen, she said. That's where it closed off. Everything she said was a waste of time. Wendy used bagels to bring everyone together. She brought them in garbage bags. Everyone came to the front door when they heard Wendy arrive. They knew she was coming with bagels.

I told them what I was going to do. The home, which is never a house, never an inheritance, is simply the place where you eat. I find my neighbour on the doorstep checking my mail. He takes the postcards, the letters sealed with kisses. I cherish all that is given me. Without gifts, I would perish from embarrassment. It is raining.

It was green. It was great fun. It was an open-air house.
They'd axed the walls. The ceilings were gone. The steps were
still there. They went down to the basement. In time, one of
the older boys asked U.P. what happened. U.P. looked curiously
at the boy. After a moment, he smiled, gestured. He wanted for
the boy to sit down. The boy obeyed. It was, after all, U.P. telling
him to sit down. U.P. began to tell a story. A story he had told
so often. Years before, he said. But then he stopped. One thing
was certain, he said. But then he stopped again. He stopped as
if his life depended on it. As his life continues to get sadder and
sadder, he'll stop telling it altogether.

Look at it this way: I'm here anyway. Whether I write or not,
I am here. But to write is to choose to be here where I already
am. This is something akin to what is often called the journey
from here to there. Only from here can you begin to talk about
there. From here, there does not exist. Here is thrust into there
as the child is thrust into the corner and asked to contemplate
what he has done. When I find myself there now, in adulthood,
what I savour is the knowledge that I got there despite the
knowledge gained from being here. And when I am here, I am
most alive – most vital, most energetic – when exploring my
memories of being there. These memories are so sweet that
I come to believe there is where I always want to be, forgetting
that the sweetness of the memory is inextricably attached to
the reality of being here, remembering there.

I go in the bedroom. Jorg is petting a cat. Listen, he says.
I listen. But I don't hear anything. One drop of blood is as
terrible as a thousand, says Jorg. One life as precious as another.
More precious than the lot of us put together. More precious
than all mankind added up together through the ages.

It wasn't the story and it wasn't the boy. Neither, in itself, was enough. It's the same feeling I had the first time I fell in love, she thought. It's both the boy and the story. It's the fact of a boy who can tell such a story.

10. David opened the little white gate at the edge of the world. He turned to have one last look. The beautiful garden. The little house. But it was gone. David was back in his kitchen at home. Nothing in the kitchen was different. David was a few years older. There was a cup of coffee. A deck of cards on the table. David dealt out the cards. Took a sip of the coffee. It was cold. He saw a horse fade to nothing. He saw a haughty god in the clouds. He saw a beautiful bird silently gliding by a cloud. But he also saw funny things. A big-headed baby smoking a pipe. And frightening things. A terrified man clinging desperately to empty air, calling for help, sinking into sand. David found himself on a wooded hillside. A wide-eyed girl nearby. A giant bird perched on her shoulder.

It was a can opener and it made him shudder. He looked upon it as one might look upon an omen. He lifted it in the air. It was silver. All silver. Slim. It would open only so many cans. But, for now, it seemed essential. The guy across the street started telling everyone about me. Whenever he saw me come out of my house, he'd call from his porch. He'd hold his hand up. He'd wave.

I was in love. She looked like pale death. You look awful, I said. Don't ask, she said. I asked. I had to ask. We didn't dress well in those days. John wouldn't enter a church or a ticket vendor. The gates were cast iron. The façade was dilapidated, but cold. It was on prime real estate. Full of rats. In the winter, John got me salt. He'd hand it to me over the gate. I feel bad, he'd say. It's for God, I'd say. Eventually, when I finally got around to getting that look down, I went back to see if Johnny was still around. I didn't recognize anyone, though. I had given up entirely when I ran into the girl. You look terrible, I said. She put her lips to mine.

In some ways, the step forward is painful in its awareness of itself as awareness. It isn't so much that I want to return to where I was as a child. Where I was as a child was nowhere. I had not yet been here, so how could I possibly contemplate going there. Consider childhood as a place that is no place, a place that knows no place.

A guy in a minivan asked me if I was mental. His kid was in the passenger seat. It was a cold day. I could feel the stars pushing down.

I couldn't get inside. He'd locked the door. I went to the window. I could see him. He was in the kitchen, putting dishes in the cupboard. I lay my head against the window. Felt the steam on my cheek. My eyes iced up. Men on horses arrived. Is this Francesco's place? the lead man asked. Yeah, I said. He's locked the doors. I can't get in. One of the men on a horse laughed. The lead man turned and looked at the other men. The men on horses all laughed. Then they turned their horses and rode away. There were great white clouds rising off the horizon, like steam torn off the muzzle of a horse.

He held the circumstances to his fault, the instrument in his hands. He put the mouthpiece to his lips. He made no sound. This isn't reciprocal, she said. The curtains blew into the room. Clouds scudded across the sky. Beyond the clouds, the sky was blue. Look, the man said. He picked up a remote. Clicked on the TV. He flipped through the channels. After a while, he found a war. See, he said. A man fell in the mud and bled.

David didn't wait to hear what the man said. He turned and walked away. Goodbye, the man called. David didn't hear him. He was out of the living room, almost out the front door.

Would you know? he asked. How would you ever know? I don't know, she said. You don't know how you would ever know? he asked. Or you just don't know? I just don't know, she said. Her lips looked so dry that I licked them. I did it suddenly. So suddenly that she pulled her head back and looked at me. It might have been a bemused look. Or it might have been disgust. She didn't run. Or even turn. She continued to outline her plan to achieve better sales, then went back to her cubicle to check her e-mail. Or so she told me.

Have you ever lifted your chin? he asked. No, she said. Not recently. I can make it to the bathroom and back, he said. I wash every day. Then you must know a thing or two, she said. It's when you're washing that you get to know a thing or two. You dip that cloth in the water. You lather the soap. You take a little bite of whatever it is you are currently eating.

The wind dies. He's not sure what to think. He looks at the place he was looking at all along. Nothing has changed. I made the birds, he says. You did, she says. On the train, he says. I know, she says. I worked on them every day, he says. I know, she says. It drove me crazy, he said. Everything drives you crazy, she said.

Why doesn't she eat her food? he asked. She does eat her food, she said. You just don't see it.

It was dark in the car. He had such a look of dumb longing on his face. She could see his face, yellow, in the high parking lot lights that spread their glow in uneven pools splashed onto the dark winter pavement. From that day on the girl loved him. She loved him the way she loved herself, for the startled look of awe she saw when she looked in any mirror.

For children seven to elevenish years of age, with lots of energy, usually about fifteen of them, at two o'clock, immediately outside the library, to provide activities for the imagination.

"Their belief in the Magic was an abiding thing. After the morning's incantations Colin sometimes gave them Magic lectures. 'I like to do it,' he explained, 'because when I grow up and make great scientific discoveries I shall be obliged to lecture about them, and so this is practise. I can only give short lectures now because I am very young, and besides Ben Weatherstaff would feel as if he was in church and he would go to sleep.'"

–Frances Hodgson Burnett, *The Secret Garden*

11. Three brothers sat on the sidewalk. They were wearing hats and mitts. They had finished their jobs. It was early afternoon. The sun was weak and watery. One brother rubbed another brother's face in slush. The third brother raised his hand. Listen, he said. The two brothers stopped fighting. Listened. The brother who had raised his hand was wearing a hat. The hat had earflaps. The brother pulled the earflaps away from his ears. He tipped his ear. Moved it like an antennae. You hear that, he

knew this. She knew this as certainly as a person knows their weight and eye colour. She let her hand fall from the doorknob. It hung by her side. She looked up from her feet. The boy at the front window was gone. Mary looked a moment longer into the library. Finally, she turned. Stepped off the stoop. Walked into the snow. Moved into the back alley that ran behind the library. The boy was waiting for her. He was there as she came out of the lane onto the sidewalk. It was much brighter on the sidewalk. The moon, at the end of the road, was large and orange, like the sun burning out. The boy had snow in his hair. His eyes were big and brown and looking directly at Mary.

Driven out of my own living room by witches and dogs and other short things, I heard a small sound. Shortboy asked me when he could quit school today, she said. What a sweety, he said. That's not what I said, she said. Doing a job starts by imagining the work it would take to move me from where I am to where I imagine I might be. The only real job is to die. But there are a lot of different ways to get that job done. I tried to think about nothing. I don't feel hate or love. I don't want to fail. I was cold. I was a long time coming home. Find the place of finding, I told myself. The wind blew against me. It didn't want me to get home. But I kept going. It was dark. The drizzle was turning to ice on the path. The trees seemed terrible. I got home. I was going to fill the tub with hot water. First I went to see Shorty. He was in his room. He was playing a video game. Once I have filled the tub, I told myself, I will get in. I filled the tub. But Shorty wanted to get in. I let him get in. Sorry, he said. Don't be, I told him. Just get in. I wasn't angry. Not really. There's tons of water in the world. I can't see getting worked up over it. Shorty was in the tub. I read to him for a while. He got out of the tub. I got in. He read to me. Then he left me alone. I went to sleep. I woke up. My head was tipped back against the edge of the tub. My mouth was open. I put my hands on the edges of the tub. Pushed myself up. Stood. Swayed. Stepped over the edge of the tub. Dried myself. I went downstairs to the kitchen. I ate my dinner. I did the dishes. While I was doing the dishes, I listened to Shorty. Shorty asked me questions. I kept moving around the room. I had nothing. I was waiting. I was trying to answer Shorty's questions. I already knew I would go to bed early. I knew I had to.

Your sleep of mulch, your mountain of warmth, teaching your wound by word of mouth. I got up early. Before the sun came up, I made a girl and set her down on the floor of a room I was thinking of with railings around it for no reason other than the fact that I like railings. And the girl had boobs. She was thirty. She sweated under her arms. Her sweater stuck out where her boobs pushed on it. Don't touch my boobs, little boy, says the girl. I was five or six years old. One day, I told my dad he had to go away. He'd be back on Wednesday, he told me. I missed him, of course. But I was also afraid. I'd never been afraid before. Not like this. Now I was afraid of everything. Yet it wasn't the things I faced in fear that caused the fear. I don't think it was. I think it was something else. I think it was that I brought fear with me. I sent fear out. I transmitted fear. Like a radar signal, it came back and set me to trembling. Like learning a foreign language, no matter how good I get, no matter how perfect my accent, I long in my heart to speak the mother tongue. I believed I might be deficient. I spoke the language of fear. No one seemed to understand. I came to believe that others don't know this language. You can tell when someone is lying. Listen to this: as awful as it sounds, I think I was ready to lie. I think I believed, at that point in my life, that this form of lying might be the best way. I wanted to speak this language others seemed to speak so easily. I got good at the language of lies for a while. But always I kept my ears open for someone who spoke the language of fear. I sometimes almost couldn't hear it. I sometimes almost believed that it was gone.

Last night, I got the banjo out and sat on the piano stool behind Mark. Mark was at the computer. He was doing homework. He was on MSN, too. I was thinking I wouldn't get to play much. I had this moment to play. Sometimes no one interrupts me. I really do get to play. I was playing little exercises tonight. Like the chromatic scale my last teacher showed me. And the single string exercise he also showed me. I was waiting. One of the kids was going to want something. But no one stopped me. Mary went upstairs to watch TV.

We could see the difference between the urbane and the sub-urbane. We could see how they handled their respective versions of fear. We could see these things like we could see the words on the page of a large print book. The first step toward fear is always a matter of bluff. The urbane bluffs in a different manner of complicity. There it is. We've said it. It's a gamesmanship that seems beyond the sub-urbane. Earnestness, said the old man, is the hallmark of the sub-urbane. The gamesmanship that makes the urban bluff possible is far too layered for the sub-urbane.

One of the problems this winter was hearing the social worker constantly knocking on the door and resisting the temptation to answer. On the subject of the place of literature in the city, I have no idea where to position myself.

On Wednesday, Dad came back. Somehow, though, it felt like he wasn't back. He cried when he left two hours later. When you cry, you've left already. When your heart goes on crying, even after your eyes are dry, you're gone for good.

I go upstairs to the stacks to find some Perchik. Clancy stops me outside my cubicle. He wants to package teen library programs. Do a media campaign. In the fall. Fall's too soon, I say. I sit in his office. Listen to Clancy. I try to look him in the eye. Who the fuck is actually in there, I'm wondering. Then he releases me. I eat a big muffin. I call my wife. You should see this muffin, I tell her. I want my wife to like me. I've spent almost thirty years of my life trying to get her to like me. It's taken me thirty years to see it can't be done. And anyway, am I trying to get her to like me, or am I trying for something else, some obsolete need from my childhood? So now, when I call her, because I've been angry and disillusioned, it's like when we were first dating. I feel so uncertain talking to her. She sounds uncertain too. It makes me feel frightened and warm inside.

Dad came back on Sunday. He took me to a movie. He brought me to Grandma and Grandpa's house. Grandma and Grandpa gave us dinner. Grandma and Grandpa's bedroom was the jail. The pencil was a bullet aimed for the head. I spoke cheerfully enough.

12. Maybe, on that day when each of us knows real fear for the first time, we are able suddenly to see the fear in others. It's like a new language. I heard, all around me, a language I didn't understand. A language twisted and scorched. A language that insisted there was nothing to fear. I felt confused. You have to ask yourself, Who is Loomis? Why does he appear here, in this story, at this juncture? Does he have a place? Does he fit between two other places? Is he like a piece in a jigsaw puzzle? Or does he simply hover, high above the rest of the picture, looking for a place to touch down, but never actually caring one way or the other.

Poems won't do you any good. I'll tell you that right now. They won't give you something to talk to your neighbour about. They won't provide something to think about when your head hits the pillow at night and you hear the wind in the trees outside your window and you smell the threat of rain. This is a man who rode a hovercraft. This is a colour that has no relation to his desperation.

There's a copy of Che Guevara's *The Motorcycle Diaries* on my desk. I don't remember putting it there. I pick it up. I set it back down. Clancy comes around the corner. He's talking about a consultant's report. I listen. He stands in the opening to my cubicle. I realize I'm dreading another big project. Another project that wants to be big. A project that can't whisper what it needs to say. I try to figure out how to whisper this one. Who could help me whisper the right things? I go upstairs to find Perchik. Surely he can help.

Tom was at the back of his space. He was shovelling something onto his bookshelf. I couldn't see what it was because he was between me and the bookshelf. It was then that my phone rang. I watched Tom. The phone rang again. I picked it up. It was Gip. He was crying. I had to try to calm him down. Gip, I said, try to calm down. I forgot about Tom. After I got off the phone, I had a meeting. When I got back, Tom had gone home. I went over to his cubicle. Tried to figure out what he'd been shovelling onto his bookshelf. There was a lot of crap in his cubicle. It was impossible to see what he might have added.

One morning I arrived early for work and there was Perry outside in the parking lot. Perry was throwing a full-sized car tire. His dog was running to fetch it. Perry looked up when he heard me coming. Watch this, he said. He reached into the back of his truck. Got out a two-by-four. Hit the dog over the head with it.

Trees sway in a breeze so constant it could hardly be a mistake. It was hard to believe that was his tongue. How old was he anyway? He looked so cute in his pyjamas. Yet, he was on his way to a top-secret lab in the mountains. He said, In a poem, you need to exceed the grasp of your memory. As we proceed to exhume the details of this particular poem, we will see this again and again. What about a groove? I asked. A groove is good, he said, but a groove is not absolutely necessary in a poem.

The records are wet and hard to read. This morning I tried to pull them apart. The records are stored inside the day. You enter the small room in the west wing, the residence of small university professors. Raise your eyebrows as high as you can without developing a headache or causing any injury that might, for instance, lock your eyebrows in place forever.

Shirley had to stay in Vienna. Cam announced at the second wedding of Shirley that he was getting married to Tricia. Shirley and her husband, Kip, would not be kissing to the clinking of glasses. The standard these days is for groups at tables to sing songs to get the bride and groom to kiss. But this was not what Shirley and Kip wanted, either. They wanted people to come up and tell anecdotes. This didn't work too well. Almost nobody had an anecdote to tell. A woman politician got up and did a prepared speech. Shirley's brothers both got up. They welcomed Kip into the family. Told Kip to take care of their sister. Made veiled, but vaguely humorous, threats, in case he, Kip didn't take good care of their sister. Kip's sisters, three of them, got up and sang Hey Mr. Tambourine Man in three-part harmony. Shirley's father cried. Nobody had ever seen Shirley's father cry before.

After he finished his story, he realized that, under the story, beneath it, on the paper under where the story sat, there was something hidden. Some secret. But he couldn't find it. Even when he used his fingernails, he could not even scratch the surface.

Once upon a time, my mother saw me and I was there. I was born. What is CFO? Mom whispered. She didn't want anyone to hear her. But there was no one there. Just the light from the window on one side of her face. Dark shadows in the corners. Everyone was gone. The house was so quiet.

They were in the car. Driving. The long, dry road to the ocean. With dust in their hair. They were wearing overcoats. His dark hair was thinning. Hers in waves. They looked like a couple from the fifties. She was driving. He looked out the passenger window. Whispered something. What, she said. He looked at her. His eyes set deep in his head, dark-rimmed, like tunnels. What did you say? she said. Did I say something? he said. She watched the road. There were no other cars. There were no buildings. No trees. Just rock. And dust. A slow, distant breeze came across his face. She looked at him. She smiled. What are you smiling at? he said. I was just remembering, she said. What? he said. Everything, she said. You. Somewhere, beyond where they could see from where they sat in the car, there would be coyotes. There would be something. A valley with a river. Trees. There were clouds moving slowly across the blue of the sky. I wonder where those clouds are going, he said. Or where they've been. For a long time they drove along like that, not making a sound. He whispered stories to the window, his lips barely moving. She strained to hear. They were closed into the car, glass all around, looking out at things they couldn't touch.

My son Lenny is fifteen. He still lives with me. For a while, he lived in a jar. His mother, Linda, is currently living on another planet. Someplace, sometime, a very long time ago, in a cupboard in a house where the birds sat on the sills, there were letters in a cookie jar. It's warm here, Linda says in her letters. Do you want to join me? There are great trees and little enclosures on this planet. There is hardly time to write, she writes. Lenny has never seen mountains. He would drive through the night, he decided. Be there in thirty-six hours. Not counting stops for breakfast and gas. We could stop at a truck stop, he told his father. Get some gas.

Jimmy confirmed that he understood what Megan had just said. He caught sight of an enormous stack of hamburgers in the kitchen. You expecting company, Meg? he asked. Megan shifted her feet. Scratched her hand.

When he was twenty-two, he wore his hat into the city. When she was twenty-two, her red lips uttered words she no longer remembers, utter nonsense. Our idea was to incorporate the old space, plus some new space, as yet unspecified, into two distinct roomy spaces. Each space would have another space within it. A space within a space, so to speak.

After I'd finished my story, I put it beneath the trellis, where I'd set my drink. I put the pen down on the wooden deck beside the pad of paper. Beneath the story, I mapped out a song. A song isn't necessarily a successful succession of notes. On a banjo, a song is a combination of sounds made by notes and the orientation of the fingers of both hands as they set themselves upon five strings in a series of progressions and configurations, a series of shapes and trajectories. How each hand hunts for a path as the other hand hunts for a different, but complementary path determines the substance of the song. It is the physical path the fingers follow that predicts the message. The tricks for bringing the fingers of the two hands together in a graceful progression get blurred in the sense of organization we hunger to feel. A song is the sound that proceeds from this heartwrenching progression of movement and hunger.

She walked away from Victor, down the road toward the lights. Victor waited for her to look back, but she did not. She walked as though something on her body was sore. As though she'd been walking too long. The wind picked up her hair, then

placed it gently down, exactly as it had been before. Where
am I? Victor asked. I don't know, the girl said. She handed
Victor the cigarette. She was wearing a skirt and she walked
like something was hurting her. She walked away from Victor,
down the road. On the third day after her departure, Victor
showed the new guy how to clear a jam in the photocopier.
The new guy asked Victor a question about the photocopier's
feeder tray. Is it possible, Victor asked in response, to articulate
beauty in the formation of a response? Or, better: is articulation
a formation capable of objectification? The new guy looked at
Victor. He looked at the photocopier. There was the smell of
burning toner. Is it possible, Victor asked, to edit something
that hasn't yet been said? We come to cherish silence more
dearly, having arranged ourselves for its demise. Silence fell like
a hatchet between the two men.

13. One time, he woke up and I went into his room. I sat on the edge of his bed. That would have been twenty years ago. Soon, I won't remember that. It felt then like getting hit by a truck. It felt like being struck. The way it felt back then, the way it struck me, stuck. It was dark. The dark gave a little light to his face. His face had a certain quality.

We used to call him Isosceles because of how his head was shaped. Can you imagine? I'm Al. This is my wife, Muriel. We're only here for a week. Sometimes I still spell Muriel's name wrong. Can you believe that? We had pork chops last night. Then we had something in a crystal bowl that was so cold it made my teeth hurt. Then a man in a white floppy hat lit something on fire and holes appeared in the tapestry. That was the year I got glasses. Now I can see. I could have worn jeans that day. I was going to. But then I saw the birds trapped against the sky. Like dripping paint. Stuck in the wind. Like things on strings. That purplish thing was something I spotted through the Hubble Space Telescope. The red thing was something my daughter spilled at dinner one night. That same night, Mom called and left a message. The message was far too long for the message machine. After it cut her off, I could still hear her voice. I could still see the trajectory of her message. It followed a long meandering avenue. It stayed with me long after. Rode deep into the life I was carving in the wood of my waking existence.

It seemed a simple thing to follow the path. He saw almost immediately that the butterfly was not a real butterfly. He moved slowly, staying in the light. What can the world do for Elrond? he asked. Why is Elrond even here?

Turtles crept over the bank out back and plunked into the river like stones. There were so many of them. They fell like hair. I saw spots. I put my head down. Cards spit out of the machine. It's endless, man. I'm so tired. A man searches for reason. For terror. He feels it in the most mundane of activities. He seeks to name it. To give it form. He seeks to capture what is lost. A guy takes a walk through his life. He is bewildered. He recognizes the simplest of moments. His parents' divorce. The day the pole beside the dining room table came loose. The day he lost his toy soldiers in a hedge. The guy robs these moments for his own purposes. Uses them like fuel. The guy exists today in the mundane world of day-to-day domestic life, from the skewed perspective of an underling, undermining the simplest emotions, crippled, but at the same time capable.

The one for morons looks like it isn't for morons, but morons love this stuff.

Teenagers were knocking over gravestones. They seemed to be looking for something. But at the same time, they seemed to be moving in patterns so random they were no pattern at all. A boy stood at the top of a small rise. The gravestones were in a shallow valley. The boy was near the top edge of the western end of the valley. Trees rose high above the stones. The boy on the rise called out to the racing lines of boys, Turn over every rock! Leave no stone unturned!

What? More fucking messages. I only listen to seventy percent of my messages. I don't even have voice mail. Where are your eyes? It's so easy to fall, don't you think? There is nothing simple about being at home.

The hairdresser saw, as she got closer to the scalp, a spreading topography of red. Like a map in relief. Her comb bounced when she dragged it through his hair. The boy looked down at his hands. He answered the hairdresser's questions. But he never looked up. With the hair dryer blowing, she couldn't hear a word he said. Just the low tone of his voice. A humming underneath the high, whiny whisper-scream of the dryer.

One day, Ed says, It was their disposition. Their disposition? Sandra says. Their *disposition?* Ed nods. Smokes his pipe. Eyes wreathed. Hair the colour of straw. Whose disposition? Sandra says. The funny thing is, Ed's wife, Eva, is a bright, intelligent, good-looking woman. It's your life, Ed says. Whose life? Yours. You should take a stand.

There was a little poem with dirt in it. It looked like it might be a little indoor garden. The man looked and looked. Finally, the deliberation, accompanied by a sense of accident, made the encounter into a gathering of little birds trying to fly off the page in a silent dance that only seemed thwarted by the man's intense focus.

The man across the street is a tyrant. The man at the end of the street owns two Volkswagens. The couple next door have a very clean garage. His name is Mark. Her name is Greta.

The girl I saw go into the bathroom had startled hair. There was a fierce wind blowing through that girl to be able to make her hair do that. A hard, Godless wind. The wind of a God who is nothing but wind. Avenues leading into empty tunnels. Funnelling away until you wake up from this life and slumber away into another.

Day after day, the architects dug, led by Bill "Dig-it-Man" Johnson. I believe in experiences. I believe in that special kind of communication that you get when you are reading all by yourself underwater. I believe a sunburn can change the sound of the lake on a still day and that the hum at the end of a towel means more than the towel itself. I have always lurked alone in that place where the writer captures her deliberation and ziplocks it again as the best instance of anything she'll ever encounter.

Sammy kicked at the water. His hands hovered gently over the lake. Hummingbirds. Small creatures, moving into flowers. Shortboy traced a circle in the sand with his stick.

How do you get it to do that? he asked the cats. The cats were like a series of triangles set atop one another. Pointed ears set atop each of their heads; down-turned mouths; diverging lines running diagonally down from above their heads to where their bottoms cut a horizontal line in the rug.

He was moving. Fast. He threw a glance at Natalie sitting in her office. Just a quick glance. I knew he was up to something. But I had no idea what. Tom frequently behaved as though he was up to something. I frequently had no idea what. I had it in my head that it didn't matter. Whatever he was up to. It couldn't be very interesting. Tom kept mostly to himself. Rarely talked. Never drank. He'd never actually told me he didn't drink. But Tom never told me anything.

I was in the old man's living room. There was an old woman behind the curtains. Where did the little boy go? The woman asked no questions. Out in the yard, there was a little girl. She wore a white dress with ripped lace around the neck and sleeves. The old man's house was in the middle of a large field. The field was surrounded by rows of townhouses. The townhouses were stacked against each other, full of abandoned lives. The old man was a kind of sorcerer. It was through his strange brand of sorcery that the townhouses had been kept from encroaching on his field. Now, however, there was no longer any magic to keep the townhouses away.

The boy was in a classroom. He was watching the others. Quietly renouncing his name. Hours later, he crossed a ridge in Montana with his best friend, Kip, and his horse, Hors d'oeuvre.

A librarian sees only a chair with books around it. There is no one in the chair.

Once, at a staff meeting, Tilly asked Tom if he believed in God. Tom got a look I've never seen on anyone. It was like discomfort, only not. It was like discomfort with something malignant rooted in it. The rest of us sat in silence. We waited for Tom's answer. Finally, Tom spoke. That question is too complicated to answer at a staff meeting, he said. He looked down at his notepad and doodled something. The meeting was over.

"You are not here merely to make a living. You are here to enable the world to live more amply, with greater vision and with a finer spirit of hope and achievement. You are here to enrich the world. You impoverish yourself if you forget this errand."
  —Woodrow Wilson

14. I play my banjo for an hour every day. I clip clothespegs to the bridge to get the volume down. I can play it at four in the morning and not wake my family. Last night, when I went to my lesson, my teacher said the skin was loose on my banjo. He showed me how to tighten it. Use a nut driver, he said. He went to get a nut driver. He didn't have a nut driver the right size. So I did it when I got home. The sound of my banjo changed.

A small orange cat lay on the grass in the centre of the yard. It was licking the fur on its belly. A rain-dark sky rose behind it. No rain. Yet. A girl in pigtails looked out the window. Light canted her face. Smeared it. As though the rain had come already and washed her sidewalk chalk features of light. A black cat in a tree looked down at the orange and white cat cleaning itself in the garden behind the white clapboard house. A young woman on a townhouse balcony wore a tight black t-shirt. She stood sideways, the small dome of her stomach pushed out in relief. Her dark hair strong and thick. Her eyes blackened with makeup and sadness.

When I got transferred from my job in North York Central Library to join the newly amalgamated Marketing and Communications Department at Toronto Reference Library, I had a longer commute from my home in Richmond Hill. In the closed stacks of my new workplace, the hundreds of thousands of books stood side by side on the shelves. Ten floors of closed stacks with shelves that slide on tracks across the floor so there's only one aisle open at any time. On some floors you turn a wheel to move the shelves, like you're steering a ship.

I heard a sound that couldn't be repressed by words, or expressed in words, or torn by meaning. A deep, primal sound. The harsh, toneless sibilance of God's whisper in your ear at night in that moment before you enter sleep. Forging a pattern on blue air, the skinniest twigs taper off, leaving the branches, lifting, angling against the sky above the man sitting in the yard.

After the U of T swim meet on the Sunday afternoon, Mark fell asleep on the couch. Susy and Eric came to pick up Joe. While Joe packed his things, his parents sat in the kitchen with me and talked. A boy pulled a wagon with a record player in it. Music played. In the dark angle of the building, a man's eyes peered out at children emerging from shadows. He had to read the taps, but his back hurt so much. He remained where he was, flat on his back, his head tilted up slightly, resting against the pillow of plastic. He could see the taps at the other end, his feet against the wall on either side. But, still, he hesitated. There was someone, a girl he knew, who wanted him to be somewhere later that day. He didn't, in fact, want to go. But he liked the idea that someone might want him there. He was afraid if he didn't go she might not invite him again. He had seen it happen before. If you never showed up, people stopped asking. Sometimes, someone you don't expect will touch you at an unexpected moment. Is it something inside you that flies toward that touch? Or is it something flying from them into you? Her thick, dark hair, like a forest with my face in it. Deeply lost. Foreign and profuse. Like that, and frightening you, if you let it, and beautiful as it fell away and you grasped at it to make it familiar, and lost it again in that familiarity, only to be found again in the moment you closed your eyes and remembered the smell of her thick dark hair and the feel of each strand in your blinking eyes.

A boy looks through the window at his father in the backyard. The father has a broom. His back is turned to the boy. The father thrusts the handle of the broom under the lid of the barbeque and pushes. The lid rises. A squirrel sits in its nest in the barbeque. It looks at the boy through the window. Their eyes meet. The boy is frightened. The squirrel runs. You need a great act of love – someone's great act of faith in you – to lift you. But you also need to be ready. Be ready. Be a pit. Be a fallow field. Be empty. Be nothing. The boy's father owned a piano. It was in the basement. The father tuned it himself regularly. For there were no more piano tuners in the world.

By music, I mean, simply, the sounds you hear every day atomized in the small spaces between the bones in your ears. I mean the pulse that brushes the hairs in your ear. I mean the cosmic music of plants pushing tips of green out through dark soil. The sound of worms looking at stars in the night. The clink of ice beneath miniature umbrellas with toothpicks for handles. Some of them are like doors that are wide open. Doors into fields of tall grass in the wind. With doors like that, when you speak, your words are like something sucked into a great wind. Sent to meet something. A flock of birds caught in a gust. Flipped. Aghast. And, together with your new friend, you look to the sky. Your words are like pointers to another, bigger word. Loosen up the soil of your soul. When the seed begins to rain down, some of it will take. Be blind to some things, awake to others. Because people are always poised to disappoint you. And, in your disappointment, you are always ready to grow afraid. You are always ready to lose faith. You are always ready to give up. Don't.

What are the things in your current workspace that freak you out? Mice. That smell we get on Thursdays. That guy, Bill, who hides behind my bookshelf. The hat on the hat rack that isn't mine. Lula, when she vaults over my divider.

When people play music together, what are they asking? Who are they questioning? Are they questioning their fellow musicians? Or are they questioning the music? The structure of the piece they are playing together? Are they looking at the way the structure can be toyed with, but without abandoning the structure? The structure of a piece allows a group of musicians to meet and play together. Rhythm and chord progression and melody. The musicians are looking to this idea to determine their relationship to each other. Then they work together to overcome the structure, to fool it. But it doesn't last. The next day you wake up in more pain than the day before. Full of more questions. The questions hurt to the degree that you believe the answers annihilate the questions. Think of the questions

as annihilating the answers. Think of the questions as a kind
of dance, sounding in answers. Like a kid trying to dodge
raindrops.

"Generations come and go but it makes no difference. The sun rises and sets and hurries around to rise again. The wind blows south and north, here and there, twisting back and forth, getting nowhere. The rivers run into the sea but the sea is never full, and the water returns again to the rivers, and flows again to the sea...

Everything is unutterably weary and tiresome. No matter how much we see, we are never satisfied; no matter how much we hear, we are not content. So I saw that there is nothing better for men than that they should be happy in their work, for that is what they are here for, and no one can bring them back to life to enjoy what will be in the future, so let them enjoy it now."
—Ecclesiastes

15. His hair travelled toward the back of his head in wayward curls. Before it dropped over the edge of his head, it changed its mind. There was a pixel in the corner of the screen he sat before that looked like a strong man questioning his own ability to lift

something. The death of Tyler was a manifesto, a copy of its own derelict inability to froth at the right moment.

The book arrives in the mail on Friday. I'm away with Mark at a swim meet. I find the book on the kitchen table when we get home Sunday. It's packed and padded in a brown envelope. It's midnight. I put the envelope in my knapsack. The next day at work I open it. I pull the book out. Open the cover. Read. The spaces are divine. The space is what animates the word. The ramp from the space to the word is already word. The transition is in the mind, the step from silent meaning to intent. The noise of intent floundering suddenly in the silence that surrounds it.

The swim trip was this weekend. On Saturday, Mark swam all morning. He made finals in two events. So we went back in the evening. In between, I was feeling crappy. I took a tub at the motel. They had a great tub. Much better than the tub we have at home. Mark went out while I was in the tub. Called on one of his swim friends. Joanne. They went out with a couple of the other girls for a walk. They wound up in a pawn shop. Mark saw some CDs he wanted. He came back and got some money. Went back and bought the CDs. On Sunday, Mark made finals again. He was in the last event, the 400 IM. He'd already swam three thousand metres that weekend. Fifteen hundred metres Friday afternoon. Almost a thousand today. The pool deck was practically empty. Just Mark, eight other swimmers and their coaches. In the stands, eight sets of parents. A couple of little brothers. Some sisters. Three lifeguards and twenty timers. Mark looked pretty tired. He was standing by himself, on deck, waiting for his turn.

There are things we have to do in between the things we don't have to do. The things we don't have to do are the things that keep us hungry. Don't ever confuse the things we don't have to do with the things we have to do. Don't ever confuse our terrible hunger with our need for food. Success has to do with the space in between. How the space in between can buffer the non sequitur. Is the non sequitur a kind of failure in a world where sequence is everything? Where story is used insidiously, insistently, to redefine the moment? Is the space a place among non sequiturs where you can breathe? A place where you can re-breathe the idea of success as it stands in the non sequitur moment, waiting for us to decide how to make of it something more than what it appears in the moment to be?

The women in their cars like lights, like stars dipped in sky, like celestial wind scurrying down Yonge Street. Turn right. Disappear.

In the end, the music became so overproduced it lost its humanity. Even at live shows, the bands were so scripted, so mechanized, that living beings were hardly necessary. Music became a set of numbers. With the mysterious fragility of humanity gone from the music, people lost interest. Not in music per se. In music as they understood it from what they heard on their computers. Music wasn't banned or forbidden. It wasn't outlawed. It was simply taken for granted. That's what happened to music. Music belonged to everyone and anyone could practice it. This was democracy at its most transparent. Many songs were spoken, or growled. Music was machine produced or fully scripted, blurringly fast or aimless and meandering. Musicians were either achingly devoted to perfection or utterly untrained. There were no musicians left who pursued their vocation in an effort to walk out the back door of technical proficiency and rediscover the exuberant innocence that makes a child's song so achingly poignant. The boy's father had been a concert pianist. When the sort of music he created seemed no longer to have any audience at all, he became a lonely soul in a basement tinkling out little tunes on a broken piano that he had to tune himself.

On Sunday, when no one was looking, God made a couple more things. He was sitting in his backyard resting. It was threatening rain. He looked up at the sky, took a sip of the drink he was nursing. He thought, I can't just sit here anymore, I don't care what I said about Sunday.

She worries that the buildings aren't where they should be. That we aren't where we should be. That I'm not where I should be. That we are maybe where the buildings should be and the buildings are maybe where we should be. Think of it this way, she says. The buildings are over there. And there. And look. Look over there. Now look here. We're here. You see? John saw a building made of little stones. He thought of things you could put in a lunch bag. Ridiculous things. Things too big to put in a lunch bag. He thought of a side of beef. He thought of things he had seen on TV. If you listen hard enough, you'll hear the spaces in your life.

God had married by this time. He'd had kids. He was driving a little Honda. But it was not big enough for all God's stuff.

The boy was ahead of the man, calling him to hurry. The man moved slowly. As though each step required an absorption of thought so great as to be uncontainable. As though each step were the result of every moment thus experienced in the life of the man. Later, in the evening, they walked together, side by side. The man and the boy. The sun behind them. Arriving eventually at the park. It was the man who folded his heart.

I'll put my book in my knapsack and turn off the light. I want to catch the night before it leaves me here, alone on the floor.

Ron pulled open the door. Stepped onto the sidewalk.

Looked at a red car. It drove away. Ron looked at the sky. Nothing. Blueness. Ron crossed Yonge Street. Some girls walked past. Ron looked at the girls. They looked at something behind Ron. Ron turned. Looked where the girls were looking. There was nothing there. Cars. Buildings. A bicycle locked to a bicycle post. Ron turned back. Walked. It rained. Ron got wet. He walked. He turned. Went in a door. Stood at the counter. Looked at a woman's back. The woman turned. Can I help you? Could I have a coffee, please? Just cream? Sure.

16. Most of what the man played now involved ancient-sounding melodies tapped out gently by his right hand, accompanied by single note or dyad-based counter-melodies played by his left hand. The boy heard this music come up through the floor of the little house they lived in. The music seemed to rise with the heat from the furnace, tinkling like musical wind from the register at the base of the wall next to the head of the boy's bed. Sometimes the boy would sneak down to the basement. Find a place to hide. Watch his father play. Watching his father play gave him nothing. So the boy just listened. He laid his head on the rug. He hid under the green corduroy couch. The boy remembered seeing the way the father sometimes crossed his left hand over his right to play a counter-melody pitched higher than the melodies patterned by his right hand.

Tutti and the boy drive the car out of the driveway. There is rust around the wheel wells. I can see the rust when the car gets out on the road. It turns sideways to me and I can see the rust as it pulls away. The people across the street wave. They sit on their front porch and wave. I wave back. Tutti and the boy wave at me. The boy yells, Bye, Daddy!

My sister's cat, Truly, died in somebody's basement. Stopped eating. My sister was living in England. I was driving a school bus. I was living in a one-room apartment. I can't remember where my mother was living. My mother moved further and further away. Then, one day, she came back. I guess Truly got lonely. She'd lived with one member of the family or another for sixteen years. Then, suddenly, she was living in some stranger's basement. I picture Truly sitting on a milk can. One of those old-fashioned milk cans you see in people's apartments. Sometimes they fill them with dried bulrushes. When I picture Truly, this is where I picture her. Sitting on top of one of these old-fashioned milk cans. In some stranger's basement. Her eyelids half-closed. Then she just stops breathing.

I go back into the house. The house is empty. I sit in the empty kitchen. There's nothing left to do. I've done everything. I did it all last night. I made my lunch. I laid out my clothes for work. I don't have to go to work for another hour. I sit in the empty kitchen. Listen to the house. There are no sounds. I listen to how quiet the house is.

Whatever it was I was doing, I just kept on doing it. It was something different from whatever it was I was doing before.

There are various kinds of music, the old man told the boy. I knew a girl once whose music existed for all the wrong reasons. Music can ennoble, the man said. But it must be capable of the basest motivations in order to resist and rise.

In the lab, the old man layered the chemicals. Mixing things in approximate quantities is not a science. If you get a little bit wrong, it might even work to your favour. You layer your understandings over future events. Your words might be more or they might be less. Each a trigger for something you can gauge, but never predict. Each a moment followed by another imperfectly gauged event. I want you to think about this the way you might think about a secret. You hear someone whisper. You can't hear the words. You know there is a secret. You don't know what the secret is. Someone is telling someone else a secret. You're in the same room. You hear them. But you hear only the hiss of a whisper. You can't hear the words being whispered. Most of us want to keep the secret. Meaning what? If we write, does that mean we want to keep the secret from ourselves? It's a secret we don't want to face, isn't it? The secret meaning is something about ourselves, something we don't want to believe about ourselves.

Is there somewhere, under the ground, where you don't know exactly where you are? So you don't know quite where to begin digging? But that doesn't mean you shouldn't dig. Does it? It just means you might want to be prepared to do some hard work when you decide to start digging.

The guard at the cargo pass didn't look like an average guard, but maybe no guard looks like an average guard. This guard was tall enough. But skinny. Like a sapling that's sprouted up too quick. He looked willowy and delicate. He had no bulk. No thick neck. No wide head.

I like the feeling of my feet being sore and my arms being sunburnt. I continue to hope that she will get her buttons out. When she gets her buttons out, she is silent and beautiful. Her eyes look rested and alive. It's like everything I need to know about her is there in the way she approaches her buttons. The way she puts her fingers in the tin. Stirs things around. The way she'll pick one up and look surprised. Like she's never seen that one before. Like she's never seen anything like that button in all the world in all her life.

The old man had a routine:
1. Wake up on back and stare at ceiling
2. Roll over onto side and stare at curtains closed over window
3. Slide body close to edge of bed
4. Drop feet over edge of bed
5. Pull back one curtain, look outside
6. Stand
7. Place hands on windowsill, stretch quads
8. Place left hand on back of right arm, stretch shoulder
9. Repeat with right hand on back of left arm
10. Leave bedroom

Things that happened after that included making coffee and peeing, but there was no set order. The old man liked to put the coffee on before he peed. But sometimes he had to pee so badly he peed and then put the coffee on.

The boy should survive in the box, the old man thought. Do not remove the tube from your arm, he told the boy. The old man pictured a tiny little truck, something you might doodle on a piece of paper, pulling up to a little tiny door. It was ludicrous.

17. He made pizza. Saw Joan outside the window. Joan was under a tree. Her chunky hips. Her purple lips. The oven was on. He could smell garlic. Onions. Joan breathed. He could see her breath. It came out of her mouth. Hit the cold air. Turned to steam. Joan stamped in the snow. She was by the big tree, the streetlight behind her. Her frizzy hair a halo. Hands in pockets. Eyes dark. He opened the oven. Pulled out the pizza. It smelled hot.

I'm going down, I said, hold the rope. If he lets go, I'm gone, I thought. But imagine if he doesn't. I'll have made it further down than anyone before. And when I come back up, I'll have this knowledge: someone was willing to send me down and then, unexpectedly, bring me back up.

They knew not the purpose of the flies that landed on their food. They went to it with hearty appetite. They had not seen each other in so long. I hate these lusty flies, said the boy. As do I, said the old man. They vomit in your food, you know, said the boy. So I have heard, said the old man. And have you heard that they breed disease, said the boy. Obviously, neither wished to spend this precious moment together talking of flies. And yet, the talk went on. Did you know they have faceted eyes? asked the boy. This, also, I have heard, said the old man. They ate ancient cheese washed down by questionable water.

It seemed to David, now in his seventeenth year, that his father had displayed a kind of proud regret at the size of his hands. David had seen his father's idols on TV. White devils with large hands. Bird-like, fluttering over keys. In *The Wizard of Oz*, Judy Garland walked a fence. The fence was the rainbow. Sound cascaded beneath her voice the way the fence cascaded beneath her feet. She struck each note with a pure intensity of emotion that wasn't in the song when David's father played it. When David's father played Over the Rainbow, there were extra notes all over the place. Like flies on a horse's ass. David's father seemed to wait until it was too late to rescue the next melody note from the chaos of his playing. He sometimes didn't bother to rescue the next melody note at all. David felt a terrible fear in these moments. He waited to hear what his father would do. It seemed utterly irrational. But then, quite miraculously, David's father would pluck notes out of the air that caused a sort of redemption. David's father somehow made it seem like every note was exactly the right note. David would feel rescued. What he felt was like a victory. His victory, not his father's.

I wasn't going in unless she came out to get me. That was what we said she should do. When the time came, she should come out to get me. I thought of knocking. I didn't want to knock. I didn't even want to go in. I realized there was a God. It was one day last July. The temperature was in the hundreds. I was reading a book. I suddenly understood that God was dead.

18. I leaned on the wall between the men's and the women's washrooms. I was holding my book. A man in white shoes came out of the men's. A woman with tall wispy hair went into the women's. After a time, she came back out. She went down the hall. Turned a corner. I didn't see her anymore. I hid the book behind my back. I didn't want to read. It was nearly eleven o'clock. My morning was shot.

She came out looking all lovely. It's awesome, she said. He's got a gift, don't you think? Did you see that movie where the man came home on the train? They got an Olympic athlete out as a guest speaker. One who had won two gold medals. So all the politicians were talking about a double gold effort. Making a double gold effort. An Olympian effort. That sort of thing. We were all out there in the square, listening to these politicians. Councillors, actually. City councillors. Each of these city councillors had some comment to make. All of us have to go out there and make a gold medal effort, they told us. All of us had on costumes. The guy who was the leader of our team had made up signs. Little eight and a half by eleven inch signs, nicely coloured, and he had come around and taped these signs to our chests. He stuck four pieces of tape on each person's chest to hold the sign on at all four corners. The Olympic athlete got up to the microphone with her two gold medals hanging around her neck. She told us she could see how committed we all were by the simple fact of the costumes we were wearing. She was talking about all the other teams. Teams who were actually dressed up in real costumes. Not like what our team leader was telling us is our costume, which is an eight and a half by eleven inch piece of paper with four pieces of tape on the corners.

It's easy to look happy for one picture, I told Cleo. But she wasn't listening. She was hearing something altogether different, a noise like a saw in the distance. A saw so far in the distance that it isn't the saw you hear anymore. What you're hearing now is the distance pressing down on you like an outer wall. Like a wall of water, making your ears feel thick and your hair go wavy.

I saw the vacuum cleaner saleslady trying to sell some guy a vacuum cleaner. I was there to pick up the bed frame. There are some scratches on the car doors. Sammy likes to unlock the car doors for us. He likes to unlock a door and say, There you go, Daddy. Shortboy was down playing games on the computer when Sammy and I got home. Sammy went in and sat down at the piano. He played Deck the Halls straight through without making an error. Years ago, a bunch of old men (he didn't say how old they were) sat on a mountainside with the scent of burnt grass blowing a breeze through their beards as a solitary bird high above screamed its piercing cry. John watched Sammy's fingers and arms move with the motion of the piece. When Sammy came to the end of the piece, he stopped and sat on the bench a moment while everyone clapped.

I was born somewhere and ever since then I've been growing up and things have been happening. The breeze has been picking up, like swarms of bees growing angrier at me, until it's a full-fledged wind blowing, scattering bedding, roof tiles, pig troughs, patio stones and some small animals. A woman has touched her cornstraw hair, saying to the men who stop to talk to her, Think of it as the sun. My parents are no longer living together, which, on the one hand, was a six-year-old's dream. To be able to make a distinct differentiation between the one parent and the other. The Chinese man is holding his cigarette with his thumb and forefinger, the way you see men in movies hold their cigarettes. He's looking at me through the smoke from his cigarette. I decide to take a shortcut through the store, instead of going around the outside. The quietness of the vacuum cleaner was not its major selling point. It was not a quiet vacuum cleaner. She touches her cornstraw hair, thick as it is with the sun, ropey marionettes hung from the clouds by wind. The wind picks up like a swarm of bees bending the yellow flowers. The woman bends with it. Don't worry, she tells the men who visit her. But it isn't me who worries. She wants to take the pink flower, but I'll take you instead since Dad will like you better and Grandma and all the penitents will give you water.

19. Even as he gives himself over utterly to the signs of another existence, he is aware of the fact that he is breaking the rules. Even in those moments when he is most thoroughly absorbed in the stories painted by the words between the covers of those books he chooses to broach, even as he gives himself over utterly to the written signs of another existence, even then, he remains on some level inescapably aware of the tenuousness, the sheer danger of his position. Like the planet Saturn, with the bulk of her existence concentrated in the spherical globe of her main body, yet always encircled by the bits of matter that, when taken individually, amount to nothing, but when viewed as a conglomerate entity betray an unmistakable and surprisingly deceptive single entity; just so, even when the bulk of his consciousness is caught up in the throes of a gentle or calming passage of poetry, he feels encircled in this ring of danger.

It has a mystery where I come in writing. I jump out. Look! I say. There is no way of knowing when a lot of things or nothing is going to happen. When Sammy says stop, I stop. I want to tell my story. Listen. I remembered talking to a girl on a beach. In California. She wanted me to send her a postcard. I didn't mean anything by it, he told her. I thought maybe you didn't want me to have any of that spaghetti, she said. She looked like she was going to cry. I thought maybe you wanted me to fix something for myself. Why would I want you to fix something for yourself? I've got this spaghetti here. Why wouldn't I want you to have the spaghetti? I don't know. I just thought maybe you wanted me to fix something for myself. There's a lot of spaghetti, I said. Why wouldn't I want you to eat the spaghetti? He went back in the living room. Started sorting CDs. He was putting them in alphabetical order. By artist. After a while, he couldn't sort his CDs anymore. He went back in the kitchen. Why wouldn't I want you to have any spaghetti? he said. What possible reason could I have? You didn't say anything, she said. About the spaghetti. When I first came in and put my things down, you never said anything about the spaghetti. I just wasn't thinking about the spaghetti. That's all. I was thinking about other things. I had some things on my mind. Okay? I know I didn't say anything about the spaghetti. When you first came in, I had other things on my mind. I didn't mean anything by it. He touched her arm. Okay? I thought maybe you wanted me to fix something for myself. She had black mascara and she was looking at her shoes.

She said I should call her back in November. Call me in November, she said. I said okay, I'd call her in November. She said I shouldn't worry. I won't worry, I said. She was just busy, she told me. That's okay, I said. At the moment, she was very busy, she told me. But things would get better, she said. Things should be better in November, she said. There is no rain of meaning, I said. Nothing for the space inside.

I yelled at the house. The house was dark. Bastards, I mumbled. I slammed the gate. It shut. Who left the gate open? I wondered.

Mom would borrow my sister's scissors. She never went out and bought a new pair. She often described the old pair of scissors. I've had them since I was a child, she would say. They were a gift from my mother. I loved those scissors the way other girls loved their dolls. They were long and shiny and they'd cut through anything.

Sammy was crying on his pillow. He was on the floor. When I was that young, I was the same. I had no idea what was in store. My pillow might have fallen off the bed. It might have seemed like the greatest sort of tragedy. It might have been enough to set me to crying. You're a little bugger, I tell Sammy. No, says Sammy. I'm Sammy. I'm two. No, you're a little bugger. No, Daddy, I'm not a little bugger. I'm Sammy. I'm two. He got the ketchup out of the wool sweater. He got a decent dinner on the table every night for a week. He had to keep looking in the mirror, having little conversations with himself.

Dad visited us kids on weekends. He bought us ice cream. He took us to movies. He let us play minigolf. Then he'd take us home. My sister would get out of the car and go into the apartment. But I'd stay in Dad's car a while. I'd tell Dad about Mom's scissors.

One day, I went out and got scissors at Grand & Toy. I took them home. Here, I said to Mom. Here's your scissors. They've been down in my room all this time. Mom looked at me. She looked mad. She looked like she was going to cry. Her face looked weird. Like it didn't know what to do with itself. Take them, I said. Where did you find them? she said. In my room,

I said. Under some clothes. They've been there all this time? she asked. Yes, I said. Ten years? she said. Yes, I said. And you couldn't find them? No. Bullshit. You were hiding them. She took the scissors and went to her bedroom. I could hear her crying.

My dad and I played tennis once. Part way through the second set, Dad looked like he was going to die. It was hot. His blood sugar was down. I wanted to tell him we should quit. But he kept playing. When the game was over he sat on the bench for a long time. He was trying to catch his breath.

Imagine it is our favourite book you are holding. What is the main idea of the book? What would a person be looking for who was reading the book? What would they hope to get? A certain fold in the curtain, where light comes through, and shadows of things behind the curtain are obscured. This, of course, is what we are looking for. But isn't there going to be more? And how have we decided this is our favourite book? Is it well within the scope of our understanding. Is it well written? My favourite book is a letter written by my mom when she went away for a year and only wrote to me once. Come home, she wrote. But I was home. It was she who must come home at once. Is it simply the latitude the book permits? An unwavering path of prose. The last bit of imagination is the hardest to let go of. A writer provides precise directions. You are commanded to imagine your way. All you real breadwinners can ever hope to provide are guideposts. Dimly perceived candles in the ganglions of jungle that are the last vestiges of this man's imagination. He must die.

You have chosen your book in the silence of an empty library. As you turn to go, the pages become lost to you. Here are the words of your chosen writer. Here is the sound of something you have caught. You hear something. Or perhaps it isn't something you hear. Perhaps it is something you become aware of. Something you believe you have become. You lift your eyes from the book to listen. What was it? The faint rustle of clothing on clothing as a body moves. An increase in atmospheric density. A subtle smell. Another person enters. The sphere delimited by the range of your senses contracts. You feel the presence of another. You're not sure. For a time, you stand still. You focus your attention. Your imagination is running wild. There is indeed another person nearby. Who was your dad? the old man asks. A cretin, the boy says. Thirty-two years old. His eyes were pink. At a certain point in the day, the cat needs coffee. Don't give up, the father says as he strokes the creature. Don't give her coffee, Dad, Mary says.

20. Even as this moment stands between rows of bookshelves, manifesting the immobility for which bookshelves are known, he imagines shelves that float side-by-side like beats of a heart, or boats beyond a break wall on a day when a storm is coming, boats waiting to re-enter the harbour, and, in their haste to make their way through the narrow breach in the wall, the captains of these many ships have allowed their vessels to drift much too close to one another. Imagine yourself between these unstable shelves, controlled by ghost helmsmen, battered by the collective storm of their contents, and you hear a sound. Do you know what the sound is? Yes, you do. You've been hearing it all your life. And, although you've denied it all your life, you have known what that sound is about since before you can remember. You know exactly what this sound is. You know so well that it is like breathing and thus negates itself as something so utterly familiar as to be beyond ready definition. This sound rises up in you as though it originates in you, as though you are its creator and suddenly you realize that the most horrifying

sound you can imagine begins in you.

Tom's voice was surprisingly loud, like a partition thrown up across her office. It sounded like someone had stuffed cardboard down his throat. I can't come with you, anyway, Tom, she said. I've got too much to do today. So Tom went out of the office. He was thinking: I should have just asked her to marry me. It's August 23 and there was my perfect chance, and now what have I done? I'll never get married. He climbed down the steps to the lobby and his legs looked like cranes, folding and unfolding in grey flannel pants.

Isn't it true that you've got the heat on? And if that sonofabitch, that lousy, no-good bastard, tries to tell me he doesn't have the heat on, then I want to know, I want him to tell me, I want him to make it clear to me just what it is he has on. Because he's got something on, and it is making me hot.

From inside, the world looks so different. It's like ripe fruit. It's like the tips of mountains for mountain climbers. Inside me is like a range of mountains. I'm nuanced. But from outside, people see only this or that moment. Like the tips of the mountains they seek to conquer. They seek to conquer me and move on. I'm the end of a book to them. Inside, I slow down and wait and I dread the end. Every moment between here and the tip is better than the tip. The tip and the fall away into eternity. If the mission is to die, then the only way to carry on with the mission is to resist death or anything that looks like it.

Shame is the liquid that douses the flames and cools the coals.

David was forty-three. Sitting by a fire. In a shelter. Under a great ledge of rock that jutted over the track for nearly a mile. It was almost midnight. David's companions were asleep. The flames were dying. Now and then the fire uncovered a small space of unburned wood and a single spiral of flame shot up, reaching for the ledge. Falling like a string of water in a waterfall. Rising again. Falling.

I'm fine, I say. Just fine. And I smile. And they like it when I smile. They look my way. They say, There's Howie. He's smiling again. They nudge each other. They giggle like they are little girls, when really they are old ladies. Even the ones who aren't so old look old. They look tired. They have lines around their eyes. Their mouths are puckered up, covered in lipstick. They have great hair. It hangs like straw. Some of them tie their hair back. Their faces look severe. They've seen too many groceries pass by on their conveyor belts. The same things pass by every day. Over and over. There's nothing new. Sometimes, the customers have twelve or fifteen cent coupons. They hold them in their fingers like they were gold. Sometimes, the store will get a new line. For a while, the cashiers will notice the green boxes popping out from among the milk and eggs. Like bright little boats in a choppy dark coloured sea.

It was too big for him to see the far side. There was nothing unusual or unnatural at the bottom of the ridge as far as he could see. It was a dust bowl. There were no trees or bushes. Just miles of red soil. He went back down to where Dudley was tied and stood by the horse for a while. After a time, he spoke. What do you think, old boy? he asked the horse. Dudley pawed the ground. Tossed his head. The man laughed. Patted Dudley on the nose. Something doesn't feel right, the man said, his expression suddenly serious. I can't put my finger on it. It's got nothing to do with this month. The air is too still or something. And, indeed, the air was very still. The man was afraid it was going to rain again. He headed off to find some wood. He looked up at the sky. Saw dark clouds racing by. And still not a breath of wind on the ground. The man cursed himself for leaving dinner till now.

I watched the weather station for an hour or so. There was nothing else to do. I had time. I might have read a magazine. I ate a bowl of cereal at one point. Drank a cup of coffee. I chose a coat. I went up the street. Got rained on. Got on the train. On the train, I thought about work. I wouldn't want to talk to anyone when I got to work. I'd want to let everyone know I was tired. Sick of all this shit. The weather network. The endless cups of coffee. The train which brought me here. But everybody else would be tired, too. They wouldn't want to talk to me anyway.

21. Mom calls me at work to tell me the manuscript is gone. Stolen, she says. Stolen? I say. Yes, she says. Stolen. Just then Hannah comes into the staff room. Hannah sometimes bites her hand until it bleeds. She comes into the staff room and tells Alice to take off her boots. Alice always wants to know what you had for dinner and how you made it. I call Gordon's office and talk to his assistant. Finally I call Gordon at home. He wants to know if I can get him a woman while he is in Toronto. I ask him where my manuscript is. He says Leon Rooke has just written a pisser of a novel. Is that good? I ask.

The boy was very white. His freckles stood out. But even his freckles were pale. The paleness of the freckles made the boy's face look unfocussed. There were lines between his eyes, above his nose. He came to the library with Claudia on Fridays. One of the librarians began telling everyone she knew she suspected the boy might have AIDS. Outside the library, death was a huge, black vista, continuously becoming.

You have to think of yourself as two people. One of the

people you are is doing things for the other. The way to convince yourself that anything you are doing is important is to be someone suddenly aware of the importance of what you are doing. You are doing what is important. You are watching. You are hammering. You are making a table. You are sawing. You are repairing your life.

People need to feel as though there is something that needs to be done and that someone is watching and appreciating the need. But no one is watching. There is only you alone in the heat beside the field of flowers. Ignore the sun. The rain. The world tipping into another day.

How can they do that? How can they give up everything – I mean, call in sick and everything? How can they live together in that tiny place? Spend all their time talking about him? How can they live like that? It's like they're a projector. Everything they do is a projection. It's like there's no roof or something. Okay, look. It's just – you know – they don't see each other. Every now and then, maybe. I mean, and then it's like, I love you. I'm sorry. I've been absent for the last twenty years, but I'm very sorry. You know, they live somewhere else. In their jobs. Whatever.

This is the story she told when she was alone at the kitchen table and her father was in the other room with his hearing aid out. The wind was blowing hard outside, whistling in under the balcony door. For some reason that always scared the girl. She hated to be inside. She touched her hair. As though her hair might be the source of her fear. As though her fear might be there, hiding in her hair. She touched her hair tentatively. Then she pulled her hand away. The sun was going down. When it got all the way down, the sky felt clear. The sky shone straight in through the kitchen window and touched the girl on her hair.

So I went out. I walked over to the park. Earlier in the day it had rained, but now the sky was clear. The sun was shining. The air was clear. It was like the air was encountering a series of windows, negotiating them in such a way as to arrive, finally, where I was standing. The sky sent its light to me at certain angles. The lighted angles made the dark shadows somehow darker. The wind didn't seem so bad. Now and then a gust sprang up. Skittered across the pond. Caught the tops of the trees. Tossed them. I sat down on a bench. Under a light. It wasn't quite dark. But it was going to be. Soon. I took out my notebook. Started to write. Pretty soon, an old man came along. He sat down beside me. I looked over what I'd written. I was woefully sorry I'd ever come out here. The old man was looking at his hands. His hands were wrinkled. Bony. He had them folded in his lap. He was wearing a dark trench coat, matching hat. I was about to get up and leave. But then the old man spoke. Are you a writer? the old man asked. No, I told him. Oh, he said. I thought you were. I was over there, on the other side of the park, and I saw you over here, and I said to myself, There's a writer. I looked at the old man. I shrugged. There were some sores under the old man's nose. But his eyes looked familiar. As though I'd seen them before in somebody else's face. Somebody I knew. I looked at his eyes. I am a writer, I said. The old man nodded. I thought so, he said. I guess it was the notebook. The old man nodded some more. I'll tell you a story, he said, and you can write it in your notebook. For a moment, this seemed like a great idea. I clicked open my pen. But then I started to get nervous. I didn't want to listen to this old man and find out his story. I unclicked my pen. I closed my notebook. I have to go, I said. It was colder now. I got up from the bench. The wind was blowing from the direction of my apartment. I put my notebook down on the bench. Started

Looked inside. Now the sun could no longer touch her. Her father could no longer see her. She was alone in the cold halo cast by the light from the fridge.

It was midnight in the subway station. It had been raining. The pavement outside was wet. There were a couple of kiss-ass men in suits coming up out of the hole in the ground where the subway vomited its passengers into the night. A man and a woman sat on a bench in the kiss-and-ride station. They were kissing. The woman's name was Jodi. The guy she was with, Merton, was sitting close to Jodi, his leg touching hers. David and his father were on another bench. The kiss-and-ride was round. It was a glass building with stairs in the centre that led down to the trains. The stairway was a drain. It was like those nightmares where you're hanging onto the edge of something, trying not to fall, and below you is the void.

Whose point of view is it? the girl asked. Can you switch points of view that way? It's depressing, J.S. said. Our professor was J.S. Smedley. He had a movie in theatres. The professor last year said to choose a single point of view, the girl said. He said first person was easiest. I can see the three old folks with a can of peas and an old couch, said J.S.

Say you could use only body parts to describe how you felt. Coming up the dirt path. The bus raising dust in the distance. I looked down at my shoes.

A guy goes into a classroom. Hair greasy. Face unshaved. He touches his chin. His eyes look like lakes. He looks at the blackboard. The messages there. He understands nothing. What does it mean? The guy goes home. The bus. The wind. Little poofs of cat hair, like angel breath, flow toward the vacuum cleaner and disappear up the hose.

The thing Mary thought she was slithering toward fades

away and Mary stands up. She thinks she has been asleep. It is three o'clock in the morning. Mary opens the window. Across the street are the other houses.

PART 2

1. The customer was on the verge. He wasn't high up, but he forced himself to feel as though he was. He looked down and forced himself to feel vertigo. He squatted down. He was forced to use the glass of his binoculars to try to start a fire. He spoke to the man behind him. Said: I'm walking away now. Said: I'm never returning. One day he could see everything. The next day, he was lost. He tried reading magazines. He tried drinking coffee. He felt overwrought. We don't want to see people, he said to the wife. I don't have any desire to see people, said the wife. We don't want to see them sitting in their kitchen, he said. We don't want to see them strolling hand-in-hand under well-groomed trees in the sunshine, she said. We don't want them rushing home after work, he said. We're switching our allegiances, she said. We're not to be bullied, he said. We will keep all our messages to ourselves. We will hide our messages on pads of paper, written in pencil, or written in ink. This will be at our discretion. Pencil or ink. We will decide at the last minute. No one will be able to anticipate the outcome. We will

not be influenced one way or the other. Not by money. Not by promise of great power. One day, I will love again, he thought. But the wife...the wife...I'm not sure about the wife. There had to be some way to come out of this. There comes a time when no man feels regret. Look, he said. But it was over before she could raise her chin and look. It was no longer a matter of looking. Everything was escaping. Little by little. He recognized nothing except his mistakes. Does this make sense? he asked himself. He looked at himself in the little glass he used for shaving. There is everything, and then there is nothing. Start with everything. Start with chocolate. Start with cream. Start with stones in pails. White stones that shed their powder. Clipped green grass. Start inside. You should try to see. And then, when you do see, when you start to make the outline of the thing come alive, and you begin to believe you are about to see the thing fully, look away. Quickly now. No time for nonsense here. This is not a game. Inside, there was a woman. Inside the house that no one could see. There was a woman, and there were things none of us can imagine. Push your face close. But you still won't see. But still, push your face close. You can't know if it will or will not be worth it. When it's over and done with, when you're old and close to death, you'll see the mist of the face you pushed. You'll have that misty outline in your eyes. You'll have the mouth. The nose. Those few stray hairs that make a halo around the head. Know that someone might be watching. From the house over there. Or from above. God might still be watching. His muffled voice speaks directly to you, a dent in the centre. The roar of the truck engine downshifting on the highway. The spectre of mountains in the black space at the back of the mind. That moment when you try to get inside and you miss and fall and the falling never stops. Between us, we own nothing. Let us practice. Let us touch each other. But only in practice. Let us not get serious. Let us not get serious about anything. Let us brush each other accidentally. Then walk in opposite directions. We'll never see each other again as long as we live. In New York, this is possible. Your life will come back to get you and you won't be there. You will never win anything. You have never considered somewhere to be anywhere you want to be. I would have done anything to help you choose a place and call it somewhere. Filaments of wind touched your eyes, like probes trying to see into your brains, trying to find out the motivation of the common earthling. The light caught us and froze us like a moment remembered. We ate. We ate well. We ate broiled meat and baked potatoes and instant pudding. When we got back, we could smell the gasoline and sense the very real omnipresent potential for explosion. I wanted to explode. I wanted alchemy. Bread would become toast. Water become ice. Cars would skid, becoming fish as they rolled and drifted sweetly to the bottom of the river. The hollow thump of enclosed capsules dropping into the sediment at the bottom of the river. Trod upon moments breaking the surface, submerging again. So quickly, we're not sure what we saw. Not sure we saw anything.

From upstairs, a man begins his descent. I married a woman named Mary, he thinks. There's a white house with a concrete addition. The addition was already there when the people moved in. Good morning, Mary mouths at the window. She shakes her head in despair. They need salt and a thousand other ingredients. There are things they want to make. Are they ever going to touch that place they once aimed to touch? When the fridge comes on, Mary knows that is her cue. She ascends the first step. She cannot yet be sure where this will lead. Although it's a safe bet it will be somewhere upstairs. I'll take that bet, the man thinks, as he reaches the halfway mark on the stairs.

I used to run like hell to catch the GO bus up to Richmond Hill. I'd get off the subway, race through the tunnels. I was trying to beat my old time. Each day I would do this. I would run up the long flight of stairs to street level. As if by magic, there was always a bus there. I was always amazed by my luck. I started to notice things. Like, if you got in the first car of the subway and you were the first one out the door, you could be the first onto the escalator, the first through the turnstile, and, in this way, you could shave a few seconds off your time. Every day, I ran up those last few steps into the station wondering if the bus would be there. Every day, the bus was there. As though waiting for me. As soon as I stepped into the bus and dropped my money into the coin box, the driver closed the door and pulled out of the station. As if he'd been waiting for me. I bought myself a stopwatch and started timing myself. I developed a rigorous training regime.

In my version of the nightmare, I have a bicycle clamped between my legs. I'm holding onto the edge of an open manhole. I know there's no bottom to this manhole. I don't want to let my bike go. But, in the end, I know I'll have to in order to save myself.

The girl and the boy were planning. Away from each other, they had their own plans. Together these plans fused, like two cars meeting head-on on the highway. Together the girl and the boy felt. They were getting sucked down a drain. They felt the slip. The last thread of anything they could hold onto.

They met at doughnut shops. Three men. They had coffee. The father talked. We're still a family, he said. We still have our love to show. Show your love. Their love was a magnet. It

2. The one thing I won't pick up out in that parking lot is dead birds. I figure that's someone else's job. I'm not sure whose job it is. But I don't think it's mine. If I see a dead bird in that parking lot, I just leave it there. Right where I saw it. I don't even report it to anyone. I don't even know who I would report it to. If I wanted to report a dead bird in the parking lot, I don't think there's anyone I could actually report that to. Once, I saw a shoe out there. I didn't want to go over and pick it up. I'd seen shoes out there before. Never one that small, though. This was a very small shoe. My feeling was, I shouldn't go over there and pick up that shoe. But it's my job to pick up things like that. So I went over and picked it up. I held it in my hand. Turned it over. It was size zero. I imagined the baby whose shoe this was. I wondered if I should keep the shoe. Take it home. Put it on the windowsill in the kitchen. Beside the plant above the sink. I get sun mornings through that window. The shoe would be there when I did the dishes before packing up to go to work.

I finished drinking my orange juice. I went upstairs. Got

back in bed. Tutti was asleep, but Sammy wasn't. He kept rolling over and kicking me. He did this for about two hours. Then he went to sleep. I could tell by his breathing. I was thinking about getting up. But then I went to sleep. When the radio came on for me to get up, I threw my arm out to shut it off, but it was the wrong arm and I smacked Sammy in the head. I apologized before I managed to wake up. I had the radio on too loud. I shut it off. Tutti and Sammy were still asleep.

I had a dream. In the dream, I was trying to catch a bus. I was telling Tutti I had to catch a bus. This bus came only once every hour. I couldn't afford to miss this bus. I kept telling Tutti how important it was that I not miss this bus. Finally, I just went out and caught the bus. It was right there when I got to the bus stop. I was amazed. I got on the bus. I told the driver I was glad I hadn't missed the bus. I smiled a big stupid smile at the driver. He smiled back. He said, There's another bus comes along every five minutes. Everything fell into place at that point in the dream, so I woke up. They say these dreams happen in a matter of seconds. I believe it is a spatial-representational thing. Something in the brain. Some memory gets triggered. The entire space/time reality of that memory is actualized simultaneously. It sure as hell seemed like more than a couple seconds to me that I was standing there trying to convince Tutti that I had to get out to the bus stop and catch that bus. It was a commuter bus to Aurora. I've never in my life taken the commuter bus to Aurora.

Scattered throughout the castle were spaces where sunlight pooled. On the floor. Across the ceiling. On the rugs. The chairs. The tapestries that hung on walls. In the early morning and the late afternoon. It was early autumn. The days still seemed long. The sun came for hours and seemed like it would never stop.

Then dusk fell and the sun was gone. People came to the castle. They sat in places where the sun would arrive. The people inside the castle hardly moved. There was something cooking in a large pot. Steam rose. Someone stoked a fire. No one in the castle knew about the man on the bottom of the steps outside the kitchen. The evenings were warm. This bode well for the man. If he spent a night out in the cold, he would die. He was damp. A small girl watched him. Silent. The courtyard within her expanding. This girl sought warmth. She craved light. But light of a particular slant. But how is this a story? the boy queried. Say nothing, the woman told him. Check to see, she said. Sit still, eyes closed. Head tilted. Mouth slightly open. Intone words. Find words that seem not related to one another. Words that seem in no way a story. The light should be like something new. Something unexpected. The girl was glad. The queen was requesting an audience. Where would the girl go for lunch today? There was no direct sunlight in the corner where she slept. She was glad the queen could not see her when she slept. Generally the girl's presence in the middle of the day was an animal thing. She glanced about nervously. The kitten skittered about. Someone approached. The girl's hair was tangled. Dirt smudged her face and bare legs. Her dress was a rag. She owned no shoes. She spent her days searching for light. Objects sprung out at her. Because of this, when she found such light, something inside her sprang out. Whatever it was she'd discovered that day, among objects she'd encountered countless times, she found herself, at night, feeling powerless and afraid. Her dreams were not quite nightmares. They filled her with dread. Left her flying in her bed.

A girl swept hair into piles. The girl wore a blue smock. She swept the piles of hair onto a yellow pan. She took the yellow pan through a door. When she came back, the hair was gone. Some hairs were still on the floor. In the corner, where the sink was, the girl had missed some. Paul could see them from where he stood by the counter.

Debt is a thing worth summoning. Settling back, lifting again in a never-ending rhythm with no purpose.

The father asked David to meet with him. David didn't truly believe in the resurrection. The family must have held him to his promise. He must have held out some hope, still, after all these years, for when his father called, David went. The father believed that once you were sucked down the drain, you would never be seen again. In one way or another, it would be the end. So the father stuck out his hand. David went along. He stuck out his hand, too. Their hands touched. The father said it didn't matter what they said, as long as they were there. This would be enough. In the end, you went down into the subway. There was no way around it. Maybe you went with another guy. Maybe you went alone. David and his father watched people go down into the subway. They appeared out of the dark, stood momentarily in the light, then disappeared down the stairs and they were gone. Until they were gone, they got to hang around in the parking lot for a while. They got to say some things. They didn't know what to say, mostly. They had to make things up as they went along. They had to start from scratch. They had each to get into their own little car, eventually and drive away to their separate destinations. You might come back eventually. But it won't be you who comes back. It will look like you. But it won't be you. You'll have two kids. You'll have lived in England. Or Vancouver. Then you'll return. You'll always be afraid for the kids. You'll live out near a lake. When people think of you, they'll think of the lake. They'll picture you out in the middle of the lake. They'll see themselves on the shore and you way out in the lake. They won't get any closer than that.

I like to go to sleep at night, he said – and, again, he had his hand down his pants and his mother swatted at him, cursing him to get his fucking hand away from where it shouldn't be. I can tell the story of my life between the time I fall asleep and the moment I wake up, he said. I can tell a thousand thousand stories. I can tell the story of this planet, this universe. Good night, his mother said, giving up on her mission to keep his hands away from where they ought not to be.

Whenever I see Jerry, I feel better. More alive. Less pained. I get on my bike in the rain. I'll see him next year again. The dark clover of the sky covers me over. The suffocating dew. Will felt encrusted in dew and the smell of pine was like the final nail in the coffin.

Wake up, Litre said. The two little ones woke first. They shed their hearts just by what they held in their faces. Come here, Litre said. She wanted to pinch their cheeks. She held back tears. There was something painfully bright about the morning. Something sparkling, like sun on water. And the sun hadn't even crested the horizon.

What happened then was that Mary became suspicious of the porter. Why me? Mary asked. You must have had other people come up here before me. Thousands, said the porter. Some of them must have asked to go through the door, said Mary. Almost all of them, said the porter. And you told them all no? Mary asked. This seemed ludicrous to Mary. Somebody has to be the first, said the porter. But what makes me the right person? It isn't that you're the right person, said the porter. It isn't that at all. It's that there is no right person. Am I changing my mind? No. I'm just accepting it as a thing that is going to

3. There was a disinclination to believe that we had funnelled our lives to this point. Everything hinged on a well-dressed woman who reminded us less and less of God every time we saw her come out of her office. We flocked around the Crystal Springs water tank. We each held a damp, far-off look on our face. We all knew something the rest of us all knew. When my turn came, I relied on two or three well-developed themes. I attempted to force certain situations into these themes in order that I should resonate credibility.

The father took the son to the library. Put him in a program. The program room was in the basement of the library. The books were upstairs. The father wanted to go up and look at the books. But he was worried. He wondered how the child would survive. He sat on a wooden bench in the hall outside the program room. The walls were painted concrete blocks. The lights were fluorescent. There was no one else in the hall. The other parents were gone. Their voices had echoed off the walls, then tapered away to nothing. The father could hear children crying. He stood up from the bench. Went over to the door. Looked in the little window. The son was sitting on the floor. He was putting together a puzzle. The father stood by the window. Watched. The librarian came to the door. Looked out through the little window. Looked at the father. Their faces were close. Separated only by the little window. The librarian opened the door a crack. Poked her head and shoulders out. The father could see a name tag. It was pinned to the librarian's dress. Mary, it said. He'll be fine, Mary said. You go upstairs, now. Get some books. Or a movie. Go upstairs with the other parents, now. Go. Just make sure you're back by three o'clock. Now go.

Sometimes, the right book drifts up and finds itself in your path. You pick it up. You open it to the right page. Your eye falls upon the right word. You follow the flow of the sentences truly, the way driftwood follows the surface of the sea. And then, finally, you close the book at the right moment. You look up. You see.

Sleep came quickly but didn't last long. When Mary woke shortly after midnight, she asked herself, Is a girl a poem? Is her body a letter? Are her eyes the vowels? Is her hair an s? Are her fingers little f's? Mary awoke completely. Sat up. Dropped her legs over the bed. Lay her face in her hands. She thought she might still be wearing her pretty summer dress. She touched the hem, felt the frill. She lay still. Felt something flutter in her chest, behind the bone above her eyes. She tried to close her eyes. The effort it would take seemed monumental. The fluttering shifted, like something melting, dripping across her skull onto her cheeks. A tear sprang to her eye. Like a cock going hard, it rolled across her cheek, dripped onto her pillow where it was soaked up, gone, a tiny patch of moisture hewn into a stain of salt stitched into a pillowcase like some hidden message, so well hidden it could only be a lie.

Am I really all alone here now in the wake of her passing? Five minutes later the oven timer dings. Time to eat dinner.

Maybe reading is a way of falling. I want to fall. I want to let go of everything. I want to lose everything I believe in that props me up. But falling is scary. Maybe the books I like pull away the things I believe in. Maybe they induce a fall. What people call resolution might be something an author proffers at the end to stop the fall. Anytime I gather enough courage to fall, I reach out to make sure there is something there to save me. But save me from what? From falling forever? From hitting the ground at high velocity? I don't know. I always grab onto something.

He wore his darkest pants. The night swallowed his legs. His white shirt floated above the lawn. He said something to the woman. The woman was walking next to him. He was such a serious bastard all the time. The woman was close enough to see his legs. Even in the dark, with his dark pants, she could see his legs. A cloud covered the moon. There was no light anywhere. The woman said something. He couldn't hear what she said. She was trying to be funny. He knew from her tone that it was supposed to be funny. He tried to laugh. His laugh frightened her. It was a flat laugh. Wobbly. Like an old pancake. An old pancake covered in dirt. It wasn't the pancake that frightened her. It was the fact that a man would carry such a pancake. It was the fact that a man would show the pancake to someone. The woman giggled. She felt nervous. The man will think I'm insane, she thought. She felt insane. Out in a dark field. Alone with a man she didn't know. She couldn't see the features of his face. She knew he was a kind looking man. Thin. But not harsh. Nor angular.

He thought he might touch things. Feel trees. Cold on his feet. Like being in a dream. Or an art gallery. You could see things. But they wouldn't be real. He'd look into pictures. He might think they were lovely. It might seem almost as though he could walk into pictures. Touch beautiful faces. Turn to tell the woman beside him what he was touching. The woman beside him will be gone. He will turn back to the picture. He will be the picture. Waiting. He will look back at the world. The magic will be gone. The beautiful ladies will be gone. He remembered his mother. He felt terror in his heart. He felt a sense of loss. He realized that his mother was not there. He cried out then. He recoiled. As though he had been struck.

He was out of the book without really even meaning to leave. Once out of the book, the weight of the text off him, he felt lost. He had caught a glimpse of the book and it was something more monstrous than he had imagined possible. For it was not monsters he saw gazing out of the book. What he saw gazing out of the book was the open mouths of words unanchored, adrift, hopelessly purposeless. He thought of the work he did writing publicity. He feared the worst. He decided he should enter another book. But this time, he determined, he would be more careful about which book he chose.

I cleaned my drawer today, he said. What did you do? I drove to Oshawa with a bolt of fabric, she said. How was the air? he asked. Was it that quality where you could touch it? Like, you have the car going, the windows shut, the heater on. You're warm. You hear the trucks going by. But muted. You feel you could reach out the front windshield and touch the air. The air seems thick. Or visible. Like streamers. Did you open the window? he asked. I delivered a bolt of fabric, she told him. What about the birds? he asked. I got lost in an industrial zone, she told him. Did you see the old man on the corner? he asked. The old man who was afraid to step off the curb. Unwilling to turn back. Facing the longest journey he's ever faced. What the fuck are you talking about? she asked. Exactly! he said. Ha! You are funny. Ha ha. Ho.

In the days before God or Jesus, if you thought you were dead, it was true.

What is this place? he asked. Last he remembered, they'd sold him ten tokens for the subway. It's a token of something, said the man in the booth. A token of my heart? he asked. The emptiness filled him. He slipped between notes of an arpeggio, landing gently on F sharp minor. You want lunch? Am I dead? No. He woke. Hung his legs over the edge of the bed. Rubbed his face. Looked through the window. What time is it? he whispered. His lips felt dry. Sore. The sky outside the window was grey. His heart pounded like pots being banged by those bastard kids down in the kitchen. He closed his eyes. The sky was gone. All of it gone. He felt no temptation to reopen his eyes.

Some cows were hit by a train. This happened on the outskirts of Calgary, near the foothills of the Rockies. It was very quiet. It was autumn, but the weather was more like spring. The sun was shining. The cows were gentle sonsofbitches grazing on the train tracks in a small wooded copse in a warm breeze. The breeze caused the tops of the trees to sway, mottling the ground in a pattern of sunspots that sparkled like sun on a lightly chopped body of water. We were eating pizza in a Pizza Hut outside Calgary. Tutti was talking about how hot it was outside. I can't stand this heat much longer, she said. Where is that bitch with our other pizza? she said.

4. Raoul got out the big pizza pan. He opened the fridge. Got out pizza dough. The pizza dough was in a bag. A clear plastic bag. Paula was in the bathroom. She was giving Little Scub a bath. Raoul spread the pizza dough. He pushed down on the ball of dough. This made the dough spread out toward the edges of the pan. Each time Raoul lifted his hands, the dough shrank back. Each time the dough shrank back, Raoul put his hands back down into the dough. After a while, the dough stayed out toward the edges of the pan. But it wasn't round. The dough looked like a map of North America. Raoul kept pushing. He was trying to get it round. After a while, the dough got a hole in it. Fuck, said Raoul. He could hear Little Scub howling in the bathroom. What's going on in there? he called. What's wrong with Little Scub? I'm bathing him, Paula called. Raoul flicked the switch on the radio. Nothing happened. Raoul looked at the radio. He smacked it with the palm of his hand. Nothing happened. Raoul looked at the radio. Then he looked at the plug. The radio wasn't plugged in. Paula had been ironing in

the kitchen again. She had unplugged the radio to plug the iron
in. The radio wasn't coming on because it wasn't plugged in.
A-ha, said Raoul. The plug wasn't in, he said. He laughed. He got
the plug. Stuck it in the wall. He shook his head. The plug wasn't
in, he told himself. I thought the radio was broken. When all
along it wasn't plugged in. He looked down at the pizza dough.
Good enough, he said. Okay. What next? He stood by the pizza
dough. Rubbed his hands on his apron. Not this song again,
he whispered to himself. This song is always on when I turn
on the radio. It pisses me off. He went to the cupboard. Got
a can of spaghetti sauce. He went to the drawers by the oven.
He opened the top one. Got out the can opener. He opened
the can of spaghetti sauce. The can opener wasn't a very good
can opener. But for some reason it worked really well on this
particular can of spaghetti sauce. Raoul got the rubber spatula.
The rubber spatula was in a big plastic cup on the counter near
the oven. The big plastic cup had other things in it: a wooden
spoon; a silver whisk; a plastic salad serving set; two plastic
spoons; a plastic ladle; other things; too many things; they were
sticking out at all angles. Raoul poured spaghetti sauce onto
the pizza dough. He pushed the sauce around with the rubber
spatula. This caused the rubber spatula to turn orange. It was
already a little orange from other times Raoul had used it to
spread spaghetti sauce on pizza dough. It was Raoul's job to
make pizza. It was his only job. Only he could make the dough
spread out on the pan properly. Making the dough spread out
is too hard for me, Paula once told him. If it were up to me
to make the pizza, she told Raoul, we wouldn't be having pizza
for dinner anymore. Little Scub wouldn't eat pizza some nights.
Other nights, he ate two or three Scub-sized pieces. In the old
days, Raoul used to chop real onions for his pizzas. But then

one wanted it. I liked the boy from the mailroom. He did his job, but, at the same time, you could tell he knew his job made no difference. If he did his job, it was because he believed that doing a good job was the thing to do, not because he thought it would make any difference.

She tried to eat everything at once, but halfway through the meal, she stopped. She could feel how dirty her hair was. It hung corded in ropes around her face, almost touching the plate with half a meal waiting on it. She wanted some wind. She stood, turned, took three steps, lifted the window, waited. There was no wind. She went into the kitchen. She wanted to make coffee. She threw up in the sink. After she finished throwing up in the sink, she pulled the coffee maker out of its corner. Plugged it in. While the coffee was brewing, she tried to clean the puke out of the sink. The smell of cold puke mixed with the warm aroma of brewing coffee.

She let him lie on the table for a while. He kept his eyes closed. You should go to your bed, she said. No, thanks, he mumbled. It was hard to tell what he was saying. He spoke in a low rumble, all his words blurring together. Like clay before it takes a shape. She tried to pick him up, but he held the table tightly. Please, he said. Please.

Where is this place? she asked. Just south of where Dad lives, he said. Except for the heater blowing in the little furnace room on the other side of the door, everything is silence. I guess everything is south of where Dad lives now, he said. Hopefully, she said. Yeah, he said, hopefully everything isn't north of where he lives. It might have been, though. She whispered everything. She crouched down close. She put her lips to his ear. She didn't want anyone else to hear her.

I saw a tyrant waving his fist, his knuckles like sheep on

a hillside standing still. All I can hope for is an empty page, enough space to see past the mall. Every dead thing casts itself into me, then stops, stuffs me into unexpected shapes. A tree standing like a crooked description of empty space. This desk that pushes back my pen. These sad pathetic creatures like lost sheep on a hillside standing still.

I ride my bike to work. People at work think I should be scared of cars. They go by so fast. But I'm not scared of cars. I'm scared of something. Something scares me every morning on my way to work. Speed maybe. It isn't that I'm afraid to go fast. It's as though the faster I go, the closer I come to something. I never actually see it. It's like calculus.

5. My wife was sleeping. I took a shower and put some cream rinse in my hair. I wanted to look my best. I put on a pair of jeans and a t-shirt. I did some sit-ups. I looked in the mirror. My hair was wet. I drank a can of diet 7UP. I went outside.

The sun was up. My eyes saw everything. The vast blue sky. The little puffs of cloud. The almost painfully green tops of the trees. But I was immune to the pain.

I got in the car and put on my sunglasses. I adjusted the car's mirrors, tilted the wheel down. I turned the ignition key. The engine fired.

I wanted a cup of coffee. The doughnut shop was up the street and to the right. So I turned right.

The streets were empty, except for the odd early shift worker walking to the bus stop or standing in his driveway next to his car.

In the doughnut shop, there were three construction workers standing awkwardly in their workboots. Their pickup trucks were idling out in the parking lot.

I knew the day was coming when I would have to go out and take positive steps. I'd been watching for the right day. This morning had looked perfect. I was at my ideal weight. My jeans fit nicely. This was the day. And yet, these construction workers standing in the doughnut shop were making me nervous. Maybe everything wasn't just right. Maybe the vibes were slightly wrong. Maybe I should go back home now, before it was too late.

Somehow I'd got it in my head that today would be a good day for everyone – that people would see my sense of purpose and smile at me.

Every man needs to have a dream, a single thread of purpose that drags him through his life and gives him a reason to get up in the morning. A man must always keep one eye on his dream and pursue it no matter what. He must move past all the clutter and crap that life dishes out. He must accept setbacks and, above all, he must have patience, never losing sight of his dreams, always knowing that the setbacks are temporary and if only he has faith he will accomplish his dream, because in North America anything is possible.

I moved toward the doughnut counter with new determination.

Coffee, just cream, I said. And a chocolate éclair.

The lady at the counter looked at me and I thought I detected a look of respect in her eye.

Make it double cream, I said, just to hear my voice, just to experience this new feeling of authority. Even the baker turned when he heard me speak and the three construction workers seemed to notice me for the first time.

I was the stranger in their lives, the man with the aura. They would go through their day inspired by what they had seen here this morning. They would go home tonight and tell their wives about me. Their children would stare wide-eyed across the dinner table as they heard about the man who entered the doughnut shop that morning and ordered coffee with double cream.

Too much cream, I thought after I took a sip while crossing the parking lot to my car.

As I struggled to remove the car keys from my pocket, I dropped my éclair in a puddle. I looked at it and swore. I thought about picking it up. I could see the puddle water seeping into the brown paper bag. I never should have parked by a puddle. I looked back into the doughnut shop, expecting to see everyone laughing. No one was even looking. No one had noticed my fallen éclair.

I got in the car and drove back past our apartment and toward the sunrise.

Soon I was past the city limits, streaking by farm fields and passing through small towns. I drove for three hours and then stopped at a small restaurant in a little town. I decided I would have lunch and then carry on.

I went into the restaurant and ordered a bacon cheeseburger and a chocolate shake. I sat at the counter. The girl who served me was young. She smiled at me when I ordered. We made small talk. Pretty soon my burger came.

I began to gain some confidence. Out here in the country where people were happy to serve burgers and make small talk. I ate the burger and watched the girl clean glasses and peel potatoes.

There was a highway that headed north out of the town. I decided north was the proper direction. After lunch, I headed north.

I drove until I came to an ice cream place. I decided to get an ice cream.

The place was a little booth in front of a barn. My dad died a year ago, the girl in the booth said to me as she scooped. Now my mom just sits around and watches TV and I have to support her. I work ten hours a day scooping ice cream. She looked me in the eye and handed me the cone. That'll be a dollar twenty-five, she said.

I handed her a two dollar coin.

You going up north to do some fishing? she asked.

Yes, I said. Keep the change.

When I got to the next town, which was nothing but a general store and a farm machinery outlet, I stopped at a payphone and called my wife.

Hi, I said.

Where the fuck are you? she asked. I woke up this morning and you were gone. I thought you were taking me shopping today.

Today is the day, honey, I said. I woke up this morning and I knew this was it.

Oh Christ, she said.

I don't think you heard what I said, honey. Today is the day.

I heard what you said. The last time this happened we had to sell the house and move into this fucking apartment by the railroad tracks.

This is different, honey, I said, but even as I said it I could hear what was happening. Deep in my heart I knew it was really different this time, but there was no way I could explain this to my wife.

I'll be home tonight, I said and I hung up the phone.

I kept driving north. The towns grew further and further apart and the bush grew denser. At five o'clock, I turned around and headed home.

By the time I got back to the town where I'd had the burger, it was dark. I went into the same restaurant and ordered a grilled cheese to go.

I was in here this afternoon, I told the waitress. I had a burger.

That's great, Mac, the waitress said. Would you like fries with that?

No, I said.

The lady went into the back and I could hear laughter. I began to think the world was a lonely place, that it didn't matter where you were, in the city or the country, most people were bastards. I began to think that the waitress that served me the burger this afternoon had only been fishing for tips when she was nice to me.

I put some ketchup on my grilled cheese and took it out to the car. I ate standing beside the car. I was afraid if I ate in the car I would get ketchup on the seats.

When I got back to the apartment, my wife was up watching TV. She came over to the door and gave me a long hug. She repeated a joke she'd heard on Johnny Carson.

6. They loved truffles. They passed around boxes of them as they sat places waiting. Nibbling. Giggling. Waiting for Bromley and Bromide to return. They passed about boxes of themselves. I was waiting for Derek to return. I arrived early in a panel truck. I parked and waited. The street filled up. People. We weren't meant to feel this feeling. We were meant to wait one corner before where you turned to go to the museum.

I was a young girl of twenty-nine. I had been working at this job for a few years. A new girl, part-time, suggested I try another method of sorting. This was a quiet girl. Young. Very timid. She rarely spoke. She lived on a book truck behind the wall. She spoke to mice. They told her secret human conditions. I felt I should give her the benefit. I allow myself one cup of coffee every evening. By the time I go home, I do not feel so lonely.

Outside, people were talking. I could see their mouths. I heard a tune. Voices. No words. It was dusk. Hawks circled a stand of trees that were locked to the sky on the distant horizon. The trees were tall. They were prisoners waving in wind.

I closed the window. Pushed towels into cracks. I could hear a
TV. I could hear the woman next door. She was walking on her
floor. I went through a doorway. Shut the door. It was April. A
baby cried. I went to get books. The books were on a bookshelf.
The bookshelf was in the basement. I wasn't going out again.
I might open a window late at night. I might hear words, then.
Sentences, maybe. Whispered flurries. The sleep has gone out
of me. I've got all the sleep I can get. I'm lying on the bed. In my
underwear. I have the window open. It's October. I can't hear
anything. It's ten minutes after three. The October air comes
in the window. Touches me. My body on the bed. The air from
the window brushing it. I can hear my son downstairs. Talking.
His mother telling him, Don't go up there. Your father is asleep.
But I'm not asleep. I am steam rising off a puddle. I am essence
evaporating. I am the thing that lifts off you like odour. It will
never come back. The next thing, I was asleep. I woke a second
time. I heard a lawnmower.

I need to piddle, said the boy. I will have to pen a response.
We picked apples. At an orchard. When we got home, it was
nice weather. I did not think it would be ideal for the boy to go
in and play Nintendo. Come hit tennis balls against the school
wall with me, I said. Shortboy hit a ball onto the school roof.
Then I hit a tennis ball onto the school roof. Shorty said, Let's
go home. When it was getting dark, I found a better wall. It was
at the other school. It was a higher wall. The roof was domed.
I was alone. I hit balls until it was too dark to see. My back hurt.

I got up. That went pretty well. I looked at the clock. It was
five o'clock. I stuffed a pillow between my legs. Went back to
sleep. Woke up. Looked at the clock. It was five-thirty. Then it
was five-forty-five. I couldn't remember the goddamn name. It
was a type of astrology. Dad told me about it. I would have to

ask him to spell it. Brad spelled Treakle Crinkle. He wanted me to buy some. I got these other cookies. Everybody liked them. Janice got a sitting with a Hindi astrologist. The Hindi astrologist could understand English but he couldn't speak it.

It was one room with some beds by a couple of the walls. When it got cold, the mother lit a fire. No one wanted to get out of bed. The fire had gone out. It was cold. The boy was trying to hit the girl on the head with a plastic checkerboard. The boy stepped back. Wound up to hit the girl.

They bought a book. They used one of those electronic label-makers to make a label to put on the book. My Favourite Memory, the label said. The man did as he was told. He climbed the mountain. At midnight, he lit a fire. He took off all his clothes. He prayed. He prayed for a long time. Things were happening out there. Cabs were making their way along streets. People were travelling to the coast. Streets wound in every direction. One street went straight. There were shops. Horses rode through parks. You could buy your dinner in the street. You never had to cook. Mist came up from the lake. It came up through dark tunnels under the street. Rising in the mist is a heavy silence. Everything the woman is now, everything she ever was, everything she is ever going to be, rises up in that mist. The mist is silence. The silence is really a sort of noise.

David was alone on a hill. The hill was near the place where they'd scattered Mary's ashes. It wouldn't be the last nice day of the year. David sat in the grass like a lawn ornament. He owned a jacket. But he didn't have it on. A gentle breeze blew. David could feel the warmth of the sun on his face. He tilted his head back.

Tutti wants me to come out back to look at the flowers she planted. I go around back with her. I touch the soil under a plant she says is dying.

7. It was just before he died that he saw the wrong turn he had made. He loved her. He saw that now. He'd seen her that night. But he didn't know it was her. It was there inside him all along. Like a noise. A hum. A silence. He saw the bend where his life took a course that it never had to take. He saw his life plotted out. A flight path through clouds. Death at the far end of the sky. A great fanning array of clouds spreading out before him. All those possible paths. None of this, of course, is true. The last thing he knew was the sound of voices. It's okay to die now, the voices said. That's what they told him. It's okay to die, they said. Now is a good time to die.

She lowers her hand to her cup, lifts the cup to her lips, sips. She licks her lips. Small curls of steam pass her nostrils. She looks like a woman who has forgotten what she was going to say. The kitchen is white. A plastic clock hovers over the sink. In the story, I am unable to escape. I am a common device. Try as I might, I cannot escape. In other stories, I have often been successful in eluding capture. But not this time. In this story, everything has already been written.

I didn't recognize you, the girl said. David was fairly certain he had never seen the girl. She did, in some indefinable manner, seem familiar. It felt like he might have known her mother, or her sister. I love this weather, the girl said. When the sun isn't quite out, but it looks like it might come out. David looked at the sky. He looked back at the girl. At the shape of her face. Behind the falling water of hair, the girl might have been a blank screen. The colour of her eyes. The colour of her hair. The shape of her nose. Everything about her a mystery. Yet, was she really beautiful? Yes. She was beautiful. The way the one eye was lost to the other. Slightly closed. The dark lines drawn under her eyes. The short hair. The elfin ears. What does it mean to you? It hurts is what it means. It hurts for me. If it hurts for you, then it must be beautiful. In a number of places throughout the book it said, variously, that the girl was lovely, that her eyes were striking, that she was comely and shapely and that she had the general aura of a nervous doe in an open field.

I had to go to a meeting. I got on my bicycle. I wanted to get there early. I wanted it to be outside. But it was red at the end of the sky. Drink coffee, I thought. Know what time is mine. I left at seven-thirty. Everything in the area of the meeting was a field being infected. I went down Bathurst Street. Hit Wilson. Went across Wilson. Got on Keele. I had to pass the place where they used to have that doughnut shop with the car in front of it.

When my wife and I were making arrangements to get married, we went to Piper Studios. My wife was looking for a dress. I hung around the water fountain. The water fountain was in the middle of a nearby mall. This was a sad time in my life. It was me that was getting married. I threw a penny in the fountain and made a wish.

It seems you need a special touch to repair wind instruments. Gino had that special touch.

When I had a final cup, I squeezed it till the lid popped off. Then I poured the pop across the parking lot. It ran like a tiny exact scale river past the tires of cars. I waited to see where the river would go.

I still see him float around. He's a ghost. Many years ago he married, and then divorced. A lot of time passed. Nothing much happened. People clapped. I don't think he even heard the clapping. He was thinking about the next phrase. He once went out on the lonely road, only to return utterly rejected. He made it softly. Barely at all.

Flo's granddaughter, Juliet, breaks down. Cries. She has never seen a person in the coffin. She sees certain things she has never seen before. She sees strange things. She sees things hidden in the moment and they make her cry. After a number of years, someone else dies. This leaves Juliet alone. She doesn't know what to say. She sits at a kitchen table. A woman holds her fingers to her lips. Another woman scowls. Looks angry. She looks like she is burnt out, but about to say something.

He stands alone in the dark hallway outside the front door to the apartment. He's not what he appears to be. He's not sure what he is. He can't go back now. But, for a moment, he imagines what it would be like if he could. Light falls through the living room. A woman standing in light. The past rushes up and knocks him on the head. Behind him is everything. And then it moves beyond him. Like wind. He sees a cigarette glow in the ether. He sees the bumps in the carpet. He understands what he cannot go back to.

The smartest thing those guys over at the mall ever did was to dig up those lousy bushes by the entrance and then plant some nice flowers there. I could pick up a pile of dog shit with this rubber glove and never get any on myself.

She's always been as tall as sunflowers. Standing in the doorway, between the kitchen and the hall. Standing between the beginning and the end of her life, she remembers watching certain events unfold, finding herself full of incomprehension and wonder. She embarks on a walking tour. She is silent and amazed. She is at the back of herself, hunting for clues. She imagines herself being watched. She imagines herself as silence. For a moment, from within her sad eyes, another person looks out. This is the watcher. She feels on the verge of discovery. She stands for a long, long time.

Is it possible that I've walked out the far end of a building I can't get back into?

We backed into the driveway of the people across the street. We said, Hey, look at this. We opened our car doors. Stepped onto the driveway. Closed the car doors. Turned to look at our parking job. Look at that, we said. We had cake. We held up the cake. We stood on the porch. We just baked it, we said. We went into their kitchen. They put on some music. They put the cake on the counter. They cut the cake. They put cut pieces of cake onto plates. Brought the plates over to the table. They gave each of us a plate with a piece of cake on it. They gave us each a fork to eat the piece of cake with. My wife pushed her fork into her piece of cake. She lifted some cake to her mouth. Her eyes looked at me above the cake that was stuck to her fork. She slid the cake that was stuck to her fork into her mouth. She closed her eyes. Mmmmm, she said. I pushed my fork into my piece of cake. Lifted some cake to my mouth. Looked at my wife over the piece of cake stuck to my fork. My wife's eyes were still closed. The people across the street were not eating their cake.

Maybe this seems a bit of an exaggeration, but I feel terribly sorry for myself today. But then, suddenly, I feel angry. Suddenly, I feel tired. Suddenly, I feel hungry. And fucking angry. Angry at platitudinous parlour ladies. Angry at unfortunate souls. I feel angry at the disadvantaged. And I feel angry at Carl. I feel Carl's endless insistence. It burrows in like a wood beetle. I feel no wherewithal to resist. I cry for the universal.

The people who live across the street like to get pizza delivered. They might get pizza delivered at ten PM. Or midnight. I saw the pizza delivery guy get out of his car. He took the pizza up to the front door of the people across the street. I was watching from our kitchen window. I'd just been watching the eleven o'clock news on the little TV in the kitchen. I got up to get a snack. I saw the pizza delivery guy drive into the driveway of the people across the street. The pizza guy was standing in the light from the porch, taking money from the guy who lives across the street. I couldn't see the woman who lives across the street. She must have been somewhere deep inside the house, waiting for pizza.

She bends like a nine, dark in her frame of light from the hall. I jump over her wall and we roll. Like a wave. Like splashing. Our souls crash across the rug.

I think I know what it's like to be in a world where words look like meaningless symbols. I think it can be a beautiful place. Frightening. But beautiful. Like standing on the antenna at the top of the Empire State Building at dusk. Like standing on the edge of a volcano. Looking down into the whirling pool of lava in a volcano. Wondering. What would it feel like to throw myself in? I want to break the chain of meaning. Use it to hang the highly literate people who string meaning around my neck. Around the necks of those few who still manage to find meaning outside the written word, inside the real world.

The people who live across the street will buy pizza from any of the major pizza places. We're talking now about the ones with telephone numbers you can never forget.

There was a bunch of things he wanted to tell his mother. He didn't, for instance, like the tone of her voice. He was planning to tell her he didn't much care for the colour of the living room furnishings, either. It was pretty early in the morning, but the sun was throwing light over things. Even if it wasn't quite over the horizon, the sun was showing promise. It was a pity. He was drinking coffee. He was on the couch. He had the spare blanket over his toes. The rug looked pretty clean. He could hear his mother in the kitchen. Every morning the birds make so much noise in the tree outside the bedroom window, he thought. I want to go outside and kill them. Yesterday, the men in the pickup truck came to cut the grass. He took a sip of coffee and went into the kitchen. How many glasses of water do I think I need? his mother said. She was standing at the counter with two glasses of water, one in each hand. She held them up and looked from one to the other.

8. There is another self, deeper beneath the surface. Boats floated overtop of where she lay. She could stay underwater a long time. Longer than any other woman on the planet. She sat under the table in the kitchen. Under the water of her life. Her father lurked. Like something deep. Something frightened and waiting to strike. It was a phantom of her father. The thing would lunge forth. It would lunge from within if she blinked wrong. There were men who could stay underwater longer than the woman. Two men that she knew of. There could be more. They lived in circles where they saw each other infrequently.

Your problem is...well, you've got a lot of problems. But one of your main problems...can we put it that way? Can we deal with your main problems? Then, when we've finished with your main problems, we can move onto your more trivial problems. But maybe we should start with your trivial problems.

A guy like me, I know that in twenty years I'll just be older.

Kim remembered all the times she'd jumped on the bed. They must have known all along, she thought. She felt betrayed.

Betrayed by the bed. Betrayed by her mother. But, most of all, betrayed by the moon. She'd seen the ivory glowing bitch shine through her window nights when she resisted the urge to jump. Nights when she lay with the covers crowding her chin. Her little eyes reflecting back the moon. Little coals. Glowing. Silently big in the empty night.

Underwater swimmers lived in circles where they saw each other infrequently. They floated into other orbits, just a little, like plasma, or doughnuts falling out of their boxes. Sudden bouts of diving. Kids ran to the edge of the dock. Timed everything. We opened our eyes under water, on our backs. It was like waking in a new world, blurrier than the world we were used to.

No one could have known what this room in the basement would come to mean. No one could have guessed at the meaning of the light in the night.

I leaned over the gas fire. It was over. I built a final triangle. I left the room. Locked the door. I was so tired. I rubbed my eyes. I whispered to myself. It made me feel warmer. Happier. I had a good life. I needed a meal. I needed a small animal to rub.

What'll you eat, Deborah? David asked. He wasn't a diver. Where did he come from? He was sweet. Young. Younger than Deborah. Deborah was not old. She would die. Would that be like submerging for the last time? Or like floating up out of the water, never to return.

But he had to get this book written. But he had no idea what to write. He'd never written a book before. He'd read books. I'll make it like those books I read, he thought. I should be able to do that. He made coffee. But he didn't start writing until forty years later. He was on a floating plastic raft in a pool in a small town in Ohio.

He wore his darkest pants, so the night swallowed up his legs and his white shirt floated above the lawn. He said nothing to the woman walking next to him. He was such a cad. The woman was close enough to smell. She could see his legs. Even in the dark pants. A cloud had covered the moon. There was no light out where they walked. The woman said something. It was meant to be funny. He tried to laugh. He tried so hard. He didn't hear what she said. But he tried to laugh anyway. He knew from the woman's tone it was supposed to be funny, so he tried to laugh.

It was after the coffee was made that the hard part began. Other people would hear your secret. Dressed in white, other people would come to help you find your way. A stupid thing to do, he thought. But we do it, anyway, don't we? We like to do it. We like to do it while at the same time breathing. The eyes are empty masters. Dead. You can put the location into them. You can put any colour you want into them. A couple years ago, I decided I'd just write sentences. Then I got so emotionally weird. I almost broke down. I licked a sentence, half sobbing. But no one noticed.

9. He put his hand on the baby's mattress. This isn't wet, he said. I know, she said. It was just his sleeper and part of the sheet. This thing could use a wash, though, he said. Can you put this thing in the wash? He held up the pad that lay on top of the baby's mattress. He put his nose to it. Man, he said.

He would sit up in bed in the middle of the night. He felt like everything was falling on him. He'd doze off and dream. He was in a big cavern. Huge. Damp. He was standing still, looking around. It got to be almost pleasant. But then he'd wake up. Something would twist inside. He would wonder what the hell he was doing having all these dreams about caverns. He would try to cry quietly so his wife would not wake up.

He tried to imagine where Mary was now. He saw her in various places. He saw her under a tree with a girl. There was a river nearby. They could hear it. He saw Mary at the library. He saw her alone. Then he saw her surrounded by people. Then the people were only kids. The kids were quiet. They were listening. There was no sound. Mary's lips moved. Her hands gestured. But there was no sound. Mary looked happy. The kids were noisy. They giggled. Touched one another. Whispered. Shouted. David saw mouths wide open. But he heard nothing. Mary sat in the chair like a mouse. She had no book open in her lap. She watched the kids. Her head moved. Slowly. Stopping. One particular child caught her interest. She moved her head. Slowly. Stopping. One particular child caught her interest.

They were both sitting on the bed. Alice was feeding the baby. Tom was staring at the wall. He's soaking wet, Alice said. She was freaking out. Tom felt scared. Maybe it's the diaper, he said. Maybe we should try those other diapers again.

David saw Mary at home. He saw empty space. He tried to fill it. He saw pictures on dark walls. Nothing framed. Children's crayon drawings held up by scotch tape. Mary shifted from one foot to the other. She was talking quietly. There was no place to sit. Mary had a smile on her face. They should put a chair there. David put a chair there. He could have a chair there if he wanted. Mary sat in the chair. A tall wooden chair. It was late evening and the sun shone into the kitchen.

That first night, the secret fairy was only a faint whisper she took for wind, if she heard it at all beyond the silence of her voices.

No matter what Tom had to say on the matter, it made no difference. If Alice wanted to get up at four o'clock in the morning, she would go ahead and do it. No matter what Tom said. You couldn't tell Alice what to do. Tom knew that much about Alice.

Back on Friday, I had this idea. Four hundred and one somethings. Somehow we managed to get ourselves on the road. We checked to see how few washrooms there were out there. Just field work really. After the pools and the sky shrinking past trees that may or may not be where you think they are, you come upon times, by your silence together, when you know you should keep your mouth shut.

Look at my hat, Sally said. I look like a boy. A dish I washed with my hands was a lid.

He sat outside the castle on the ground. Wind blew in the high grass. Across the fields, trees sprouted in groups. Here and there, in the distance, white clouds scudded. No sound. Just wind and the few birds whistling. He could hear his heartbeat. Someone must be watching me, he thought. But the world seemed deserted.

10. It would be a long tiring drive, getting out of the city and into the desert, and Lily was in her office rifling through her desk, looking for something. Tom could see her through the corrugated glass on the office door. He decided to pop in and chat with her. He wouldn't ask her to come out to the desert with him because he was going out there to get away from everyone, including Lily. But what if he married Lily and they became one soul, indivisible even in death? Think about all the people in the city, Tom thought. They march around like ants. If this were an anthill on my front lawn, I would pour gasoline on it, killing all the ants, not giving it a second thought. They bore him no malice, he knew. They had their own plans.

He looked up. Turrets. Guard walks at the tops of walls. Small windows high up in towers. Nothing. No one. He was alone.

When Lily straightened up, she was out of breath. Her hair looked like an unkempt lawn with some wildflowers poking out. Her eyes glassy. Her lips swollen with lipstick. She looked fat in the dress she was wearing. It was a beige dress. There was a run in her pantyhose. Hello Tom, she said without really looking at him. It's like we've been talking all this time on the telephone, Tom thought, and now here we are face to face and she still thinks it's the telephone.

He would go into the castle later, he decided. After dark. He would find it full of people, he decided. A costume ball. Faces hidden. Masks. Food everywhere. Chairs to sit on near stone walls hung with tapestries. String players playing waltzes. Men in white pants dancing. One hand holding their mask, the other on a lady's waist.

That morning, they tried to put the plastic lawn table together. The lawn table was a gift from his mother. They'd been getting gifts from people ever since they were married. They got a small plaster pillar that looked like a copy of the pillars on the Parthenon. It was two feet tall, painted fluorescent colours. Orange. Lime green. Hot pink.

Make a stir-fry. But girls won't eat stir-fry. But you cooked it just to pass the time.

I put a guy in a jacket in it. I don't know how I pulled that off. He was a laughing guy. He was a guy standing on the beach. He was standing in the sun. He was laughing. His breath was coming like steam in the cold morning air. Like horses' breath in cold air when the sun first tips the tops of the trees and red is the only colour you can imagine.

She said we should maybe hit his knee with a book. He might be comatose, she said. Or he might be semi-comatose. If we hit his knee with a book, she said, and his leg doesn't move, he's fully comatose. Use a hardcover book, she said. Use the spine. *Dad Says He Saw You at the Mall* was on the top shelf of the bookshelf. The cover is orange. It was easy to see. She picked it up. Hit him on the knee, she said. I took the book. Hit him on the knee. Nothing happened. No, she said. Do it like this. She took the book. She hit him on the knee. I might not have hit the right spot, she said. Nothing happened. She tried again. Still nothing. He must be fully comatose, she said. She looked at me. They say a person in a coma hears everything you say, she said, so be careful what you say. So we were careful.

Whereas, only a moment ago, I could smell this man's musky smell, now he is far off. He is at the bottom of a hill. There is a woman with the man. The woman is sitting in the sand. The woman is drying her hands. On her skirt. She has come up for air, only to find this man here, standing beside her. The woman has come to the far edge of sorrow. She has arrived at the inner edge of bliss. She has come to the place where the inner edge of bliss and the far edge of sorrow meet. In this place, a person loses the capacity to blame or to take away.

I was riding my bicycle home, just like I did every night. A guy in a minivan pulled up beside me. He asked me if I was mental. He rolled down his window to ask. He was fat. He had a cellphone he was holding in one of his hands. His fat kid was in the passenger seat next to him. It was a cold evening in the middle of winter. I could feel the stars pushing down on the other side of the minivan.

I didn't feel like eating something fried. I wanted to get out of the chair. Thanks, I said. Sure, she said. She had a little black purse. It was Saturday. Lake Ontario. Summer ferns. She went to the kitchen. I sat in a chair. I heard the opening. I heard the closing. Cupboards. Drawers. Got any gum? she called. She came to the living room. She looked at me. Her eyes fell closed when she blinked. You gonna eat that thing? she asked. I was holding something in my hand. I raised it to my mouth. Put it inside. Held it there in my mouth. I looked out the window.

Clouds rushed over the world. Like they had some place to go.

He was in his bedroom. He was at home. He was wearing his green housecoat. His hair was tied back. Without music, he was just flesh and fear on a road to nowhere. It wasn't that we didn't love him. It wasn't even that we did love him. Love wasn't the issue. I knew. Even if no one else knew, I knew. How did I know? I just knew. God had given me this power. So many insights. I knew without thinking. But I could feel them coming to an end now. The insights were coming to an end. I wasn't peaceful about it. I wasn't accepting. I didn't glow with the knowledge. Not at all. I was angry. I was disillusioned. Most of all, I was scared. I was trying to figure out how long it would take to drive to the airport. I had to get him to the airport on time. If I didn't, he would be staying at my place another week.

When he was alone in his room, he played Bach. He sat on a white wooden chair. He finished the piece by Bach. In the silence that rang beyond the ring of the strings, he stared out the window. He dreamed. He was walking. He was in a mist that stopped the noise of the tires on the wet streets. The mist stopped the screaming of children in the park. It stopped the noise of the TV downstairs. His music would be a silencing mist that rang indecisively, tremulously, until, suddenly, he decided. And then it would make itself known. And then it would stop. And right there, in the moment it stopped, he would slip away into the mist, never to be heard from again.

I walked to the end of my street. A breathtaking sunset in progress. I wanted to know what that sunset meant. I'm not talking metaphor here. I wanted that fucking sunset in my pocket.

I couldn't get inside. He'd locked the door. I went to the window. I could see him inside, putting dishes in the cupboards, throwing logs onto the fire. I lay my head against the windowpane.

I felt the cold hard pressure of glass on a winter day. I wept.

The landscape solidified as soon as she saw the boy. Tell the boy your name, she told herself. Tell him you dance. Tell him you've ridden your bicycle amongst the frightening, self-propelled vehicles, and you've emerged unscathed. Unscathed. She heard the word in her mind, like music bubbling up from the middle of a pond. The fields, she saw, were scythed. She was lying in a heap on a dry bed of grass. The sky was hardened into a washed out blue.

This Charlie Watts' house? a man on a horse asked. The man's horse stamped and snorted smoke. The man sat atop the horse like a pillar, like a wave, like a tree in wind. He in there? the man asked. Yes, I said. He's locked the door. I can't get in. The man on the horse had a sprig of fresh grass between his teeth. He turned to look at some other men on horses. There were a number of men on horses. Beyond the men on horses, white clouds rose from the horizon, like something damp ripped from a freshly slaughtered corpse.

I don't know how long I stood at the end of the street. I wasn't looking at the sunset anymore. I had no place to go. I had marched to the end of my street with great determination, and then I found I had no purpose being there. I went home.

11. The field stretched into the distance, butting wire fences that squeezed everything in. Beyond the fence, on the left, was a dirt laneway that led to a sprawling white house shaped like a set of boxes fallen off a truck. The house was shaded by tall trees whose branches swept the sky. God had provided here, it was evident. It broke Lily's heart to think of some of the things people had done to her. People she didn't even know. The lady in the yellow rain hat. The man with the briefcase. The taxi driver. The horse with its head down. By the river that day it had seemed so sunny. Standing in the meadow with that horse, Lily had felt like an inviolable room. What is that? she said to the horse, and it felt good to say it. She didn't care if the horse didn't answer. But the horse did answer. Her mouth full of hay. Lily couldn't understand. Want one? Lily asked. She held out her hand. The horse looked at her hand. Walked. Took what she was holding in her hand. It looked like something fried.

I stood for a while, lost. Totally, completely, overwhelmingly lost. You're lost, I said to myself. Then David walked up. David looked like an angel. And I don't mean that in a good way. He looked dead. You could see through him. You couldn't really see through him. That would be scary. But looking at him, you got the feeling you might imagine getting if you could see straight through someone and not be scared about it.

Wanna go for a drive in the desert? Tom asked. I have work to do, Tom, Lily said. She looked up, saw Tom for the first time. She pushed a stray hair out of her eye. Blew air over her nose, trying to get a hair off her forehead. He looks like a hat stand, she thought. A hat stand standing in the corner of my office. What do you want to go out to the desert for, Tom? It's so hot out there. I want to drive twenty miles or so, Tom said, then drive back into the city. He wanted to say something else, but he couldn't remember the words. On the edge of her consciousness, Lily remembered. She remembered someone old. Someone with a great bush of black-grey hair. His last poetically senile years. She almost wanted to go to the desert with this tall, crazy man. But she didn't want to find out what was beneath this. She could already see herself married to Tom. A trip to the desert would be preliminary. They would listen to the car radio. Pretty soon the sounds would be far off. Tom's voice would fade, the way thunder fades as a storm moves away. Tom stood like a cornstalk with a bush of dark black hair on top. Lily moved some things around that were piled on her desk. Tom seemed to sway in the breeze whenever he stood on a street corner waiting for a bus. At work, he looked like a bent post sitting at his desk in his suit stabbing at papers with his pen. Tom wanted to marry Lily. Tom was thirty-six. He felt he ought to marry Lily soon, before the end of the summer, if possible. He'd walk out of the office each day, tall as a lighthouse, mumbling to himself that he had to get going on this project of asking Lily to marry him. Someone turn and look back at the city, standing up on the horizon like a scaffold. I can think about all the people in the city. Then I can drive back into the city like a bolt of lightning ready to strike her dead.

He came out of the mist on the river. He was like mist himself. Mist in a kayak. He stopped when he saw the girl. He held the kayak steady in the white flow of water rushing past. He watched the girl. Then he let the kayak go. He shot past the girl. Disappeared again into the mist.

Her hunger stabbed at her heart and she could feel in her nostrils the dense presence of profuse greenery. She hoped that the man lived in the house. She hoped he would take her back to his year and that they would sit together under the biggest tree by the house. The man would leave her. He would go into the house for a moment. She would close her eyes and float.

She had a dream that night. She walked down the bank to the river and stood in a dress, the cold of the river on her knees and ankles. The boy in the kayak swept out of the mist. He had his arms stretched out toward her. That's when she woke. She held onto the dream, her wall against the morning.

I had been thinking about going over to the high school. The sun came out. I knew this wasn't a good thing. I tried to swallow. The sun is out, I whispered. But there was no one to hear me. I went into my wallet to get the little yellow card that the guy stamped every time he sold me a coffee, but the yellow card was gone. The guy had taken it.

12. I still love Bach, she said. Do you love Bach? For a brief time, she would forget her past, she would forget her questions. She would breathe. The man would sit. They would sip their drinks. They would not look at each other. She would lean back on the tree. She would look into the heat shimmering over fields. Everything would be yellow. The shimmering heat. The cool liquid in their glasses.

I believed in jazz. Jazz is the doctor. Jazz is the little detour. Everything in life is a detour. A detour from what? I can't say. That's the problem. I have no fucking idea what the thing is that isn't a detour. Bach, maybe? Maybe that's it. I should have followed Bach. It's too late, though.

I would stand in the garage and just feel good. The other girls would watch in envy, watch my every move, trying to see what I might have that they didn't, when what I had was nothing. It just felt good to be in the garage.

Go down and play some Bach right now on the piano. I'll help you down the stairs. Let's go now.

Everything, every damn thing he had accomplished, shed out, as though his skin were on fire. The whole world opening. He had no way of knowing which way to go. He thought he would just lean his head against the seat in front of him for a moment.

Her dad bought them a house. They lived in it. What does this mean? Nothing, if you ask me. But people like to think this means something. People like to think there's a pattern. All this has a reason, you want to say. Everything you do leads to something beyond what you're doing. Everything has its purpose. People like to believe in this. The man believed in this. He meditated.

I had a dream about dying. I don't remember anything about the dream. It's more like a feeling. Like a screen door opening. Like something far out in a field, obscured by heat. A place where everyone moves silently, mouths open, round as balls, floating away to nowhere. Not a freedom, exactly, but suspiciously like that. I started feeling again. Seeing. It died not long after. I realized, as I verged on sleep, that it didn't exist anymore. I believe that when you die everything goes away. So dying, once you've got done with it, is no big deal. It's life that's the big deal. I think the feeling was a freedom from insanity. I had to always wear this hat. If there was the slightest breeze, I had to wear this hat. The hat was like a toque, only it wasn't.

Tutti went downstairs and put some clothes in the dryer. I was in the kitchen. I could see a guy in a white shirt standing out in the road. He walked up and down the street. He stopped in front of our house. Somewhere, someone had their stereo going. I could hear this. I could hear bass and drums. A black man in an orange tracksuit walked by. He had mail in his pocket. Most people won't look at you for very long. The thumping was far off now. I wanted some long-term commitments. I wanted the apples to quit shrivelling up in the crisper. I wanted to be able to buy the ten-pound bag, because it saves you money. I opened the fridge. Took out an apple. Bit into it. Guys in sports cars often look at you like they are the real world and you are the illusion.

I still meditate, but it makes me cry. You can't meditate when you are crying, and every time I sit down alone in a room to meditate, I start to cry.

He threw the manuscript on a fire. The fire was his wife. The fire was the same thing as a wife. It was cooking his supper. Boiled cabbage. He hated the smell, but the taste was one of his favourite accomplishments.

I have no notion of the specifics regarding my impending domestic collapse. I only know that it's coming. It's been thirty-eight long years. For thirty-eight years things have gone my way. Think of it as the long, sweeping upswing of the pendulum. Thirty-eight years.

woman. I was in the aisle seat. People in other seats were looking at me, too. I tried to smile.

He looked up. Left a piece of himself in the grey, sad, hopeless sky. He saw nothing but a plate with crumbs. The scissors set askew. The hardcover book. The insides of the book torn free. The garbage pail on the floor beside the table. Everyone else seemed to have something to say to him. But he, himself, had nothing. He couldn't get the others to shut up. They'd phone him. Talk. One day, he just hung up the phone. Walked away. It's over, he said. He held up his hands, palms facing out toward the rest of the world. It's over. He locked the front door.

It is ironic. Don't you think? But don't panic. Isn't that what you're looking for?

I was in the loop. I would say it was a loop. I began where I was standing, ran north, then curled back and ran parallel to myself till I came back to where I was standing. I would call that a loop. I would stay in the loop. This would make a limit for me. There was an entire world of limits available. Some not what I imagined, I knew, but still...Bones. Places in other countries. Mud huts. I had to count these, too. I had to count as much as I could. I would look only at the well manicured. The well located. In them would be my methodology. The tracks bubble like a little blister when seen from above. But within, there is only mayhem and a general sense of blackness. Gravel and black stones and very little action. Motion, of course, considering the basis of the bubble is a form of transportation. Huge and industrial. Bound, in the end, to lurch hugely to a stop. I was in the outer loop when I saw the end. When I say the loop, though, I mean the inner loop. I followed East Avenue to East Marin. I knew it was there. I was taken by surprise when I came upon the river. Wide, compared to other things. The very thing I didn't need. I sat near the smell

of it. Smelled it. I couldn't cross it. I couldn't go back. I couldn't
stay. I was scared to leave.

He held me close. Told me I should talk to him more. We had
some music playing. Glenn Gould. It could break your heart. The
room filled with music. It swelled. I couldn't make it through the
windows, though I tried. I couldn't even make it to the bathroom
door. I stayed in that one room. He held me. Anchored me. The
music was the thing that kept me sane. The music depended on
us. The one night we had a complaint, we knew for absolute sure
that the music was ours. We left the room, then. We had to. The
music was anchored to us, but it was anchored also to place and
time. We did everything we could to arrest both. We went out to
get food. To play. But the rest of the time we stayed in that room
with the music.

Rain, you called it. Yes. Rain. There's no such thing, though,
is there? But there must be. Think about it. I mean: rain. There's
probably more than one thing called rain.

I was there that last day. That last minute. That very last
moment. The moment when his life sped past him into a future
he couldn't inhabit. His future stretched out ahead of him like
a flung elastic. That eternal moment as he crossed over into the
remainder of his life.

They were having the salmon. Some people had the sandwich
and soup combo. There were many women at the table, some
younger than others. The smallest woman stood by the wall,
petite, imagining herself into existence. An emanation. Large
possibilities inhabited her tiny being. Reaching out like a
small fist in her stomach, stretching hard against her skin. Any
combination of people are strange. Strange beyond the context.
Context ruins the quality of strangeness you come to love. You
could conceivably, then, not want to grow. You might not know

the context, history, background, circumstances. The smallest woman thought he might live until Christmas. But she also thought it would be a ruse to live until Christmas. He died in October, so he didn't make it until Christmas anyway. He was just lucky, I guess.

He sat in the back and played with an action figure. Sammy was ten. He still, sometimes, broke out spontaneously in song when he was eating.

14. He wanted to stay there quiet. Push himself into her and not see out. They sat rocking in the chair in the front room. They could see the houses across the street. The houses looked dilapidated. Everything looked dilapidated. It was spring. There was still some ice and some crusts of snow. Everything looked dirty to him. Like shit. She said she wanted to stay in that chair with him forever. It was the day after she sucked his fingers into her mouth one at a time. They were tired. He sat down in the rocking chair. She curled up on top of him. She said she had never been so happy. He was looking across the street at the crusts of snow by the curb. It all looked so awful.

As was his custom upon returning home from any place they had been, Sammy stayed in the car when Pauly got out and went in the house. Pauly went to the kitchen. He still had one eye closed. There was half a tomato on a plate on the counter. On the side where it had been cut, the tomato was rotten. Ruth was upstairs in the bathroom with the door closed. Sammy came in and the screen door banged shut. I'm going blind, Pauly said quietly. He opened his left eye. He saw clouds. They floated above the kitchen counter. The toilet flushed upstairs. Sammy was sitting on the landing, removing his shoes. Pauly walked up the steps to the upstairs bathroom. Ruth came out. Hi. I can't see out of my left eye. She looked. He had been dying slowly for the past forty years. Now he would die more quickly. There is something coming, Pauly said. Always. And there is something going. Always. The younger son, Shorty, could not be home alone. They called Ruth's parents. They dropped both kids off at their house on the way to the hospital. Pauly sat in a waiting room. Then he lay in a bed. The doctor looked in his eye. Smiled. Asked questions. The doctor left. Ruth sat in a chair beside the bed. I'll stay here with you, she said. Probably you aren't allowed, he said. She was allowed. But she didn't stay. It was very late. Pauly was asleep. Ruth went home. Got into bed.

The real problem, he said, and I'm talking about the problem that takes you out of the moment – the only real problem – is: you can walk out beyond the fields anytime you want, but there's really nothing out there. We're at the edge of it all, here. The edge of nothing. No matter how far into the world you go, you'll always be here, on the edge of nothing. He found his way out of the city and climbed into the hills. When he came down the other side, he found himself in another city. He crossed that city and came into the hills again. City after city followed, until he thought there wasn't a place where the cities didn't stretch out between the hills like the end of hope itself. When he came to the ocean, he sat down on the beach and went to sleep. When he woke, he turned south and followed the beach until he came to a place where the cliffs forced him to stop.

Fourteen layers of clothes. Two bowls of soup. All the heat she could muster. Still she was cold. She opened the oven. She turned on the iron. That's what we think must have happened. This was a long time later. We weren't there yet. The children believed their father had ascended to heaven and felt that one day he might somehow return, although the details concerning how this return might be accomplished were completely beyond anything they wanted to think about. They wanted to play. I could delve into it, if you wished it so. But it was sheerly a matter of belief transformed into something so unbelievable it might just be true.

He played that set so softly. Then what happened? He kept looking over at her. In between tunes. During tunes. It was one of his greatest sets, he felt. One of the greatest sets in history. Of course, there was no one there to hear it. The girl was tone deaf. The other guys were looking at him, like, what the fuck? He'd be looking over at the girl. The girl was giggling.

There are things worth telling, Matty. One of the older women was having lunch when Pauly entered the commissary. She had to decide whether or not to drive down from her place in the country. Attend the altered vision, her friend told her. It was Friday night. Do you remember the air from that summer when something happened? she asked. There are smells of air that I can't even begin to tell you. It doesn't even smell like the same air at these times? You should smell the air, Matty.

Shorty got up on the counter. Watch that sandwich maker. It's really hot. Pauly had pain in his bowel and in his shoulder. The worst pain yet, maybe. But he wasn't sure. Watch that sandwich maker, I said, he said. He recognized that, aside from keeping Shorty from burning himself, he was socializing the boy. Partly to get him through life unscathed, partly so that he in turn might socialize someone, his own children. The pain in his shoulder became suddenly intense and radiated into his hand and seemed then to echo back into his chest. He immediately and abruptly ceased all thought. He staggered. Waited for the pressure in his chest to subside. It was a heart attack, he knew. Some people survived heart attacks. He knew a man who had survived, was living a normal, if cautious, life. But that man had always lived a cautious life. Pauly sat on the floor. Shorty climbed down off the counter with a bowl. Can you move, Daddy? I need to get the macaroni.

Late that night, he walked her out to the parking lot. It was summer. The air was warm. Damp. Even at four in the morning, the air was warm.

15. He was fifty-five years old and had not become a great pianist. His math was about what it had been in grade six. He wrote stories sometimes. But he threw them out. So far, he hadn't kept a single one. There was a wife. There were kids. But the wife and kids were on the other side of something he didn't understand. There was a wall of happiness no one had prepared him to hurdle. He was playing Ode to Joy for the first time in more than forty years. It was a funeral. It was the final act in someone's play. He understood that. He felt himself whirled. Never as though he was in much control. The others knew the script. He played the organ for the funeral, but for Ode to Joy, he came down off the dais and sat at the piano. He played and he cried. He stopped, just as he had so many years before.

I tried to think of something to say. But there was nothing. I whispered. I was just practising. Just trying to hear the sound of my voice. Trying to hear if my voice was going to take me anywhere, or if this silence would last.

When he got up close to her, he saw that she was wearing very red lipstick. He sat down at the table. He was carrying a beer. He set it on the table. They went out to the parking lot. She got in a car with her friends. He made a sign for her to roll down her window. She rolled down her window. You wanna go out sometime?

Ross had worked briefly and dressed in jeans and a ripped t-shirt. That was okay. He wasn't going to church or anything. He parked across the street. At two o'clock he put a CD in the player. He cried, with the car window open, into the air on his face.

She thought it rather forward when he approached her, and went home. In retrospect (in other words, as she sat in her kitchen with three one hundred watt light bulbs glowing fiercely in the fixture above), she wished she had listened more closely. She wished she lived in a little town like the one Doris Parsons and Nan Brennan lived in. Someplace where there was any hope whatsoever of seeing him again. She was one of those who died on Christmas Eve, not quite making it to where the relatives had hoped in talking among themselves toward the end. Another Christmas. The last. Yes, I'm afraid so. She never did see him again.

I was a green rug and shouldn't be allowed to carry a gun. Dogs shouldn't be allowed to carry guns, she said. True, I told her. All naps lead to a hole in her ice. To him it feels like a gun. All the cows had offices. All the officers died. To him, it feels like guns are the only compensation.

We are amazed when a person of high IQ is in the madhouse. But they were always there. Their IQ got added later. It will fade away long before the madhouse goes to dust on a cloudy wind.

He was a teen sailor ready for the high seas. When the ship wrecked, they didn't find him till later, a thin stretched rack of flesh left on a beach in the summer where gulls not yet dead navigated currents and sometimes (for it was not a pretty beach) some tousle-haired person wandered lost to Jesus' blood mixed white in the stones.

It was three o'clock. He was still in a coma.

She worked in a movie theatre. Truly was the name of one of the cats. Showing was a way of naming another icon. She never cried. She sat cross-legged on the rug. Sometimes she had her chin in her hand. She liked the warmth of the sound it made when you pounded your fist on the floor.

I spun around and a fluffy was there. Now I'm twenty-eight and I'm married and I haven't caught a fluffy in a long time. Lives come and go. But me and the wife, we stay in our apartment. If you catch a fluffy, she says, go out on the balcony with it. Sometimes lick those grey bricks I've got lying out there, she tells me. I was probably going blind at one time. My wife thinks there's some deficiency in my diet. What makes her lick those bricks? I wonder. Also, eat the plants, she says. Among the many that hang above our couch is the one we call The Vegetable.

We met at the river. The guy from Providence couldn't get across. The only guy to get across was Helmut. A log happened to fall across. Helmut lost his shoe. A warthog ran along beside the river. Warthogs hate water. At the very end, the woman walked out into the snow alone. Her two daughters were still inside, doing dishes. She had a platter of cookies. She was talking to herself, her words steaming into cold air before her face. I will put the platter of cookies in the trunk of her car. I will surround the platter of cookies with boxes. There are many boxes in the truck. I can use these boxes, much like a clever criminal using hanger wire and a light socket to escape from a holding cell. One of the boxes has the blue windshield fluid. Another has the jumper cables. There are other boxes.

Each with its own objects. These boxes will keep the platter of cookies from shifting. If I drive slowly enough, the cookies will not slide off the platter. I will move through stoplights like something tentative. My existence in my car will be entirely provisional. Like a shadow caught in the corner of an eye, I will be gone. Inside, the car will be warm. Outside, the wind will continue to blow. The moisture on the streets will freeze. Other cars will take measures to confirm their own existence. My journey will become anomalous.

I was riding my bicycle home. I was afraid to die. Everything was going totally wrong. First, I got lost in a subdivision. I ended up at Victoria Park. It was growing darker. Halfway home, I started to hallucinate. I was thinking about God. I had this idea about God and bicycle helmets.

The day after he tried to sit up, he slipped into a coma.

16. At Christie Gardens in Toronto, on February 5, 2003, Norman Wheeler thanked the staff and left. It is time to go, he said. Norm would have liked you best, Virginia. Never laugh. Never complain. Worry a little on Wednesday. Life is always difficult.

I used to look for excuses to go down to the river. I knew I didn't need to go down to the river. But I tried to convince myself that I did. And when I did go down to the river, I tried to think of things to do down there. Throwing sticks, or stones. Or catching bugs, or fish. Or sticking my bare feet in the water in summer. Or sliding on the ice in winter. I tried to see myself as a guy who could sit by the river. Just sit. Sit still and look at it. I tried to be a guy who loved the river for no reason except the silver of it at noon, or the brown of it at dusk. I tried to be someone who could simply watch the river. The sparkle of it rippling in the sun on a windy day. Or seeing the pock pock pock of rain on the river on a wet day. Or the torrent of the river on a sunny spring day with the snow melting. Or the buzz of bugs over the river on a hot day. But I was not that guy. Mary was that kind of guy. And I envied her. She'd sit motionless forever, staring. She might have been somewhere far away in her head. But from where I stood, watching, she was a Zen master practicing the art of being the river. And I was never anything inside this world. I was a way of being outside everything.

The boy would tell stories. Barbara would say nothing. The questions would tumble about her head like hot clothes in a dryer. Mixing. Separating. Clumping. The boy's stories would answer none of her questions. Barbara needed stories. The hunger she felt was all mixed up. Food. Stories. The green and yellow air. But the boy was not going to take her back to the house. He was not from the house. Barbara could see this as soon as she looked into his eyes. He was as scared and hungry as she was. Barbara wondered if he had appeared here in the same way she had.

Sometimes I would hear some music that stopped me in my tracks and for a moment the pain of being alive faded and I felt myself inside the glow of who I am.

She told him they needed to meet. He heard bells in her voice. Saw horizons in her eyes. We need to meet, she said a second time. He saw wind on her horizons and heard the flap of wings in the undertones of the words that slipped from her lips into his ears, eating his head, laying overtop his soul.

The son stayed poised on the edge of the abyss. There were women waiting. They sat at desks. Stared into computer monitors. Stayed busy. But they were waiting.

Enveloped, he imagined her naked. Her belly button. Sunken treasure. Something gold glinted on the edge of everything. Go home, she said. He turned. And she was gone. But he brought her with him. At home in front of the TV he heard her voice. Outside his living room children played, screaming from fear and glee and he knew they screamed for him. They screamed to bring him through her mist and land him on the new land. They screamed to pull his canoe from the river. Stand him on the bank. See the string where water went. God sat on high, above the clouds, sending domes of rain to cover her and balance out the rushing force of his descent. He stood on the precipice and felt things coming toward him. Birds wheeled. He shifted his hat. There were clouds drifting. Beyond them, the sky reached, like something crawling. He stepped ahead. Closer to the edge. The air stood against him like a knife. Cold. It whispered to him. He walked back down the path. Little stones slipped away from his feet. The scratch of sun on his back, like a mother calling him home.

You never hear a thing but the echo of what you thought you might have heard. Whatever it was you thought you might have heard. Before you stepped out into this world, everything ran out in front of you and something solid inside you pushed back. He took his hat off. Sat on a rock. He waited. He could feel where his hat had sat on his forehead. He pushed his hair back.

Three days ago, I was up in the dollar store trying to find some Christmas presents for Evi and the boys. I went up and down the aisles. I looked at everything. But at the same time, I knew I should be going home pretty soon. It would be dark soon. The roads were wet from the bit of rain that had fallen. I left the dollar store and walked across the parking lot. I was almost at the car when I turned back and went into the drugstore. It was warm in the drugstore and it smelled nice.

Rebecca had her clothes off. He was against her. He recalled the hard thing he had felt on the wind that morning. He pushed back with all he had. Then he fell back. He heard cries from the night. The window squared off the moon's light. A streak of luminescence devoid of substance. He looked at Rebecca's hair. He walked into a lighted tunnel. The sounds of breathing were magnified and the light in an eye was a thing that could blind you.

He was a sad but very good-looking man. The two vehicles were joined at the bumpers. They crossed America that way. They touched one another at stoplights. They touched things no one had ever touched. He tried to collect something. He listened to the silence between people, waited for something to coalesce. When people started talking, he walked away. It's like chasing someone in a car, seeing the car get smaller and smaller, running as fast as you can, knowing you can never catch up, but running just the same, keeping your eyes on that shape up ahead in the dust, hoping for some kind of miracle. He saw hats. Hats twisted. Windswept tumbleweed shapes situated beneath them. He saw nothing. Nothing with a hat on top. At night, he lay in bed, felt nothing pressing down. It was killing him. Nothing.

We drove up early this morning, me and Mark, to a swim meet north of where we live. We drove past horse farms. The horse farms are big rolling fields. Short grass and white wooden fences. Big barns. White stables with black trim. Tall trees lining laneways. Trees naked but for the snow lying heaped atop branches. Trees turned from the sun, then peeking over the power lines at the edge of the world. I looked over to drink it in. Eight horses came across the field like a vision. Their eyes wild. Steam streaming from their nostrils. They ran straight for me.

He watched as the child tried to suckle himself on his own hand. The desperate hands scraped and shuddered about the face. He took the child and held it up and away from him. He

tucked the child up against his chest and took him upstairs and
gave him to his mother.

The wind blew hard. Everything in the world – the parking lot, the mall, the No Stopping signs planted in the little spots of brown grass islanded like puddles in the pavement – all of it blown back to the place where it came from.

17. Perry winked. You will die! he whispered. But no one heard. The loudness of wind precluded hearing. Loud? Did I say, Loud? Oh, yes! Bowls full of loud. Wind. Wind from the cupboard. God saw the end. Kept it to himself. So he tried. He tried again. He thought, Be glad when it's over. Be glad. Bright eyes flicked the streetlights. Was I the pavement? Was I pushing into the assholes of peoples' feet. People walked with a special spring in their step that season.

Someone had hung strips of brown paper in the trees at the edge of the wood and they rustled and popped like cymbals and tom-toms in the wind. It was warmer inside the forest where the wind had greater trouble penetrating. High in the branches of the trees tiny glittering bits of stone hung from strings tossed by wind, reflecting facets of bright sunlight off trees and the forest floor, like golden insects, dancing, dancing, never still. The fact that someone had come here and hung all this paper and these bits of stone from trees was not necessarily frightening. But it scared David. David wanted to meet this singular person he was hearing about. He imagined a young man. A man with a stern face. A poet. An artist. A man who rarely smiled. But when he did smile, his smile transformed the ether. His smile threatened to split the atom. But there was no one here. David heard what he thought. But he realized soon enough that it was actually far off geese honking.

A long time ago, there was an open exchange. Kind people hoped to have families. Other people wanted to give. We are fortunate. We are wonderfully vibrant. We have tremendous rage. We have an international reputation. Comedians come to our city. They come every day. They live in the sewers. They do shows each night beneath the city. People in the streets laugh. They don't know why. Why are we laughing? they ask themselves. This is the foundation of happiness.

The question is: where can I get a sandwich in this one-horse town? The answer: Vinnie's.

In any instance of internal communication, there are two people who need to listen. One of them isn't me. Because, as you know, I always hear music. I try to hear words. I try. I really do. I try to hear a path words can clear. But all I hear is the beep beep beep. They make a sound before they announce their meaning. I hear Rory's voice. The pitch. The timbre. The tempo. But what the hell is he talking about?

The creature had gold-green eyes and pointed ears and it made the sound of an engine buried deep in the earth. Whispering in the silence, I try to feel my way, she said. She spoke so softly, he had to yearn to hear.

I used to get a little glimpse of beauty sometimes. I'd see a tree a certain way. I'd wander around the city, suddenly feel something very strong, like something got through, and then it would be gone and I wouldn't feel it again for a while. I thought,

Oh, this is beauty. This is nice. I hope I see that again sometime. Then, suddenly, I could feel it all the time. And when I couldn't feel that, I was feeling something else. Something horrible, but something that made me feel just as alive.

Each volume was over a thousand pages long and each page was several feet square. Volume 12 was missing. Volume 21 was sitting atop of the stand, lying open at page 766. The smell of the book washed up. Mary leaned forward.

We have our own. We asked. Which is what we are on the whole. Cut slivers. You build things. You spill your blood. You bare your soul. You eat your breakfast every day. Vitamins. Lunch. You look for friends. You look for someone.

The smell was damp. Musty. Paper. Ink. And something indefinable. Beyond that was the smell of electricity, heat and plastic. A sharp, tangy, acidic enemy of the must.

Many lay their hands over the pages of books. Feel their cool cleanness, the leader intoned. Fit your fingers under corners. Bring a page over from the right, settle it on the left. Hear the almost silent rustling as it settles. The paper is heavy, meaty, meant to last.

I almost got up and left. There was a blue tarpaulin over the scaffolding. The tarpaulin was old. Battered. It was tattered. Every year they put an item in the budget to get a new tarpaulin. Every year that item in the budget got cut.

You look gorgeous, the woman said, brushing her friend's cheek. Her hair was tied back with a black ribbon. Wisps of it escaped and fluttered near her face. Her hair had a natural curl that made it unmanageable. Each morning, she tied it back. She was forever going to the drugstore to buy elastics. At night, her cat climbed onto her dresser and stole the elastics in its teeth, hiding them away somewhere that the woman couldn't find.

She lived in a little house in a quiet corner of the city not far from where she worked.

Sam stood at the edge, waiting. He pointed to his left. But there was nothing there. What was he pointing at? Where was this leading? Everyone has seen our little book. What do you think? Sam shouted from the roof. People heard. Sure. But no one was thinking.

The woman who had touched her cheek was Indian. Dark skin. Big shiny eyes. She took nothing seriously. She seemed to find a depth of joy in all things that made it impossible for her not to be happy. She grinned at her friend. Her crooked teeth were stained. She was wearing a dark blue blouse with bright red pockets on the front. She had yellow shoes. It was an unpardonable combination and it looked most comely.

The muffins tasted like mud with lemon added. They tasted like pieces of fucking shit. They blew. But people ate them.

You love this dictionary, don't you? You've gone to the library many times to see it. You got a job at the library, just to be closer to it. Many have warned you to move on, but you stick stubbornly to one place. There are many libraries around the city, but you stay at this one.

He entered the building as though a furious wind had pushed him here. Hair flung forward, eyes ablaze. He'd fought unimaginable forces and arrived where he needed to be just in time.

Good morning, Mother. The latest real time estimate was beyond the ken of Liberty. Liberty wore polka dot dresses that fell like cones about her shapeless body. It would be wrong to have a shape, Liberty said. She was afraid. Her eyes were huge and wet. She blinked and her face was made up to give her a porcelain glow. All the beauty in the world and what do we do?

We make checklists. And when the checklists don't seem to sate our hunger, what do we do? We make new checklists.

The front door had been an old split wood door. There was nothing finished about the place. There were two rooms in the small but busy structure. The neighbourhood was densely populated. Many of the residents were Greek. Others were not. The man came through the front door as though inflicting a wound on the building. The bulky dynamic of his arrival precluded closure of any sort. The hydraulic closing mechanism at the top of the door hissed as the door inched closed, bolstering the impression that Roger had arrived from another realm.

18. Old man: remain in the chair in the kitchen. Don't hardly move, please. Although the boy had not been aware of it, the old man had lifted his eyes enough to watch the boy leave. His face wore an expression of boredom resting atop perplexity. But that might have been keen interest hidden in his occluded eyes. The old man took note that the boy said nothing and left the galley seemingly resigned to the fact that there was actually nothing to say.

Roger stamped his feet. Snowflakes clung to his coat and hair and eyelashes. He gave his head a shake. Water droplets scattered as though Roger were a tree shaken after a rainstorm.

In the days that followed, the old man grew sick from having sat so long wet in the galley. What began as a small tickle in his throat developed eventually into pneumonia. For days, the old man lay rasping in his bed and the boy sat by his side, hardly speaking. The old man's chest hurt him, but he was determined to die with dignity. Near the end, when the boy went away for a few minutes, to get something to eat, or to relieve himself, the man popped a capsule of morphine. He didn't want the boy to know he had given in to the pain. He wanted the boy to believe that the worst thing a person could ever do was to give in.

Roger kicked the toes of his left foot against the heel of his right and pushed the boot off. Then he pushed his socked right toes against the heel of his left boot and pushed it off. One of his boots tipped over. It lay on its side like a dead animal at the side of the road. Roger picked both boots up and set them on the mat. Roger's boots looked big and bulky sitting on the mat next to the other two pairs of boots already sitting there. Mary's boots were black, glossy rubber, shorter and narrower than Roger's, and rimmed at the top by a white synthetic fiber that looked like cotton balls pushed together and glued to the tops of the boots. The other boots, which belonged to Ingrid, the part-timer, were tall white shiny boots with deeply tapered heels. In spite of the fact that Ingrid's boots stood a good few inches taller than Roger's, they looked like the smallest pair on the mat.

I'm going to die, the old man said. We're all going to die, the boy said. But he felt stupid saying it. Soon, the old man said. Maybe today.

Later, he tried to play the sound of what he saw from that cliff, but what came out was an echo, a pent-up animal. He tried to hear what the wind had whispered. The sound he made was ludicrous. A pact with dark forces. An invitation to evil. Hey Rebecca, he called out. But she didn't hear. The wind took his voice. Carried it over the roof, into the nether. Rebecca, he called again. But the wind was too much. He was out on the porch in his shirt. Hat in hand. He was watching Rebecca. She was way out there. In the field. She held a stick in one hand and something he couldn't identify in the other. She moved like a dancer through the coarse grass. Her hips moved in her skirt in a way that made him feel she was disappearing into a thickened swath of air. He could see the back of her head. Her hair. The way it fell. Like salmon in a waterfall.

Some men came and installed water-saving devices in the toilet tanks. Even little Sammy's poos wouldn't go down. If you flushed twice, sometimes three times, you could get the poo to go down. How is this device saving water! I yelled to Tutti. I kept flushing the toilet. The poo wouldn't go down. I'm taking them out, I called. I opened the tank. What? Tutti called. But she was too far away, no longer interested in water-saving devices. She was downstairs installing long, white flags of ribbed fabric across the width of the sewing room, just at waist level. She was lying on her back, staring up at the flags.

He didn't speak again after that. He stood and watched as Rebecca moved further into the distance. He held his hat in his hand. Felt the solid space between himself and himself. He danced. Out in the field with Rebecca. But without moving. Where was he? He heard some kind of bird. He turned. Pulled on the screen door.

I won't tell you what the songs were. You can still hear them sometimes on the radio, like unexpected surprises. Breadcrumbs chucked at you by well-meaning kids. We sat in the grass on the hill behind the school. Near the summer, when the sun was hot, the grass died, but we sat back there anyway. It was more dirt than grass. When it rained, there was mud. We'd stay inside, look out the windows at the ends of the halls. There was no way of knowing the songs would turn out to be a kind of charity.

Can you fix my car? she said. Her voice came slow and quiet, like a creature in a foreign predicament. She did things with her hands that made him want to weep. I don't know about cars, he said. Can you fix things? she asked. I can fix things, he said. Can you fix my car? she asked. There were little things he wanted to do. He tried to think the things he wanted to do. He thought deep into an obscurity that made the things he wanted mute beyond salvaging.

Some talk here about bubbles. But I am helpless against this talk. These bubbles rise up out of something I don't understand. Out of darkness. The darkness of the interior of a human body. I catch sight of them only as they pop at the surface.

You think I should go to school? He was lying on the floor, eyes closed, boots crossed. She was standing in the doorway, her body set back from everything, as though still trying to decide whether to take her first breath. You want to go to school? she asked. No, he said. Then why go? Her dark hair pulled back. Her dress falling. A tent around her body. You think I'll get what I want from life if I don't have a proper education? he asked. Do you think you will? she said. I think I already have everything I want. I feel like there's nothing left I need to get. You're fourteen, she said. You haven't got anything yet. I've got you, he said. No you don't, she said. He opened his eyes. Lifted his head from the floor. He looked at her where she stood in the doorway to the kitchen. She stayed framed in the doorway for a moment, then turned and left the room. He dropped his head back to the floor, but kept his eyes open, looking at the ceiling. There was a window open somewhere and he could feel air crawling along the floor like snakes.

I go over to the fridge and open the door. In the soft light from the fridge, standing there in my blue slippers and my pjs, I begin to grow angry. Who the fuck does she think she is? I ask myself. I get out the milk.

Visibility has been established. I am a sample. An example. Another particular reminder of the visible. I am just visible. Just.

David didn't think that it was much of a story. It lacks structure, he thought. He felt confused about the characters. His head tipped sideways. He snapped it back upright. But he'd seen something in that moment between sleeping and waking. It was Mary. He heard the places where she paused. He heard where she lost her grip. He anticipated her hesitation. The pauses were like little deaths. Characters died and were resurrected, sometimes as other characters. They were trees in a forest through which Mary walked. She saw a branch that resembled another she'd seen earlier. A bird called across the forest. A butterfly landed on a leaf. Dogs barked in the distance. There was civilization somewhere, and Mary was harkening toward it. It made David feel safe. But, also, somehow, afraid. Things slipped away, like standing in a river just above a waterfall. The tug of the river. The sound of water smacking other water far below. There was a man with a moustache and glasses in the story. He looked sweet and meek. But he took his glasses off at night and covered his head and rode a white horse.

I just want to go home. Right now. I'm just having a terrible headache and I am missing 90210. Her eyes looked clear and serious, but now an edge of nervousness had crept in. He stepped forward and licked her neck.

It's like that. I stay in bed. I'm eating. I can't get my hands on it. I don't get in bed unless I have to. Outside, I can't stand the smell. I can't forget. For the rest of my life, I'm going to have to live with this.

Getting to the other side of this field, David knew, was going to be one of the hardest things he had ever done in his life. It was an ordinary field. There was nothing to it, really. No

19. She could hear the banging of the men working outside. She wasn't sure if men needed to bang on things to get their work done, but it seemed to make them happy. Whatever their work was, whatever it was they were repairing, or creating, or tending to, the men always seemed happiest when banging. Late in the day, everyone would be laughing, and it all seemed quite genuine. It was the first really warm day of spring. It was seven-thirty PM. The men who would normally have knocked off at six PM were still wandering about pushing wheelbarrows and banging things.

At one point, they were all trapped in there. The three of them. Bill had gone first. Then he wrote a letter to a couple of the other guys. He wrote about London. About the clubs. About Brighton. Come out, he wrote. The rent is cheap. He wrote in his letter exactly how much the rent was. He wrote the amount in pounds. Then he wrote it in Canadian dollars. He put the Canadian dollars amount in brackets. He looked at what he'd written. It was pretty cheap. It seemed too cheap. He looked at the amount in pounds again.

Lyra smelled the dampness of the towel. It reminded her of something – something from the summer she saw the unicorn in the newspaper on the kitchen table. She thought of David. She held the towel to her nose. She had decided to be beautiful. One of her eyes was definitely beautiful. David said so himself. In a future that was a shiny new car, and slippery, David stood on her beautiful side, away from her monster side. She was asymmetrical, truly, but she exaggerated her unbalanced appearance in her mind till she was a comic book hero and villain all in one. Her evil dark side always in shadow, her bright smiling beautiful side smiling as men fell in love with her and she blew them off, utilizing the power of her dark side to taint her beautiful side, to the point where her beautiful side was uglier than her dark side. A bright, shiny ugliness like the glare of sun on a windshield in the moments after a car sails over the edge of a cliff, just before it hits the ground, spilling its human goo over the landscape beneath the cliff.

Are you nuts? Are you looking at Ingrid? She sits at her computer. Technically, she is on a break. Most people would not guess that she is a fashion plate. Ingrid is wearing the same heavy knit cardigan she wears every morning as she goes about her duties.

The old man didn't want to frighten the boy. Or anger him. Or defeat him. He wanted the boy to face the truth. But the boy didn't notice. He shook his head. Reached out to touch the old man's arm. The boy was close to tears. The old man could see in his eyes all the things neither of them wanted to see. The boy settled his hand on the old man's wrist, at first tentatively, but then with a firm grip. He wanted to say something. Words spilled into his mind. So many words that he couldn't hear a single one of them. Couldn't bring forward a single thought and speak it out loud so the old man might hear that he had control of himself. He felt the words in his head as a feeling of denial for the situation. He felt in the words feelings of encouragement for the old man. The words in the boy's mind held guilt and shame and condolences. And love for himself. And hate. But the boy said nothing. His silence defeated the words entirely. He heard the silence and turned inward. Finally, the boy set the bowl quietly on the edge of the counter and left the galley, retiring to his cabin, where he sat in silence through most of the night, crawling into his bed only as the rocket's fake morning threatened in the rising of the solar light emanating from the storage cells located strategically all about the ship.

Mary was not afraid of Roger. Roger was standing by the desk, divesting himself of his hat and coat and gloves and scarf. He was currently in one of his moods. Ingrid was afraid of Roger. She tensed visibly when Roger came in. But she would never admit her fear, even to herself. I hate that man, she seethed silently through her teeth.

The way to make a journey of this length, he said, is to hang yourself out like a thread of flesh in the wind. The boy did not understand, but he asked no questions. The old man did not speak for a long while, and the boy sank into the silence.

Focus on Biff, Mary told herself. Try to conjure in your mind the words Biff just spoke. What had he just asked her? She looked about the table, flushing slightly, hoping someone might provide a clue as to what was expected of her.

Hank hit the ground and rolled, just as he'd been taught. He crashed through a dry, leafless bush, smacked his wrist on the trunk of an old-growth tree and came to a stop in a small pool of mud. The mud was from a hole in the canopy above where

Hank sat. It wasn't raining now. The sun was out.

I don't think of it as a set of instructions, like a road map telling you directions to go to meet some guy somewhere he wants to meet you. That's the problem with a published work – it looks so clean and carefully prepared. You could mistake it for directions. Like an instruction manual for putting some pieces of wood together and coming up with a piece of furniture that looks the way the guy who designed it wanted it to look. What I see in it, when I manage to see past the pristine finished appearance that modern publication burdens a work of literature with, is something like a forest, one with no obvious path, just little clearings and breaks in the bush that you might or might not use to ease your passage. But never read into these breaks in the bush a system of authority – as though someone had put the breaks there for you to follow. Instead, read as though you were entering a forest with no instructions for getting through alive. You can drop breadcrumbs behind you if you want, or unravel string, or keep notes to help you find your way back; or you can go ahead and admit you're never going to get back.

He went to the kitchen. She was cooking bacon. I thought I smelled something, he said. She looked up from the pan. Twenty years later, he was searching for a sock. She was asleep in the bed. The covers down at her waist. Her shoulder pointed up toward her ear. Most nights, she slept on her side. After they had been married a few years they went out and got hot dogs. Hot dogs were a thing they could touch. After work. In a pinch. At odd and often unexpectedly inappropriate times.

end part, where it suddenly drops back to open position, gave me some trouble. I couldn't get my fingers off the strings fast enough. I couldn't get them off at the right moment to hit the open strings. I kept playing the last bars over and over. It was starting to sound better. At five to five I unstrapped the banjo. Lay it on my desk. I took off the finger picks. The middle finger was healing. It didn't hurt so much to pull off the pick. I went up to the kitchen. Put bread in the toaster. One regular. One cinnamon. I got out a plate. Put Mark's vitamins on it. I got him a glass. Put some water in it. Then I went downstairs. Packed Mark's Speedo. His goggles. His shorts. Towel. Deck shoes. Put it all in his knapsack. Carried the knapsack up to the front door. I went upstairs. Opened Mark's door. Whispered his name. He made a noise. I heard him get out of the bed. I picked up the heap of clothes on the floor outside his door. I brushed my foot along the floor to see if I'd missed anything. His t-shirt was still on the floor. I picked it up. I took the pile downstairs. Dumped it on the floor in the hall. I got the cinnamon toast out. Buttered it. Cut it in half. Put it on a plate. Took the plate to the table. Mark stumbled in. He ate his vitamins. Drank some water. He stood by the table while he drank. Then he sat down. He picked up a piece of the toast. Took a bite. I went over to the toaster. Got out the regular toast. Buttered it. I asked if he wanted jam. He said he wanted raspberry jam. I put raspberry jam on the toast. I cut it in half. Took it over to the table. Put it on his plate. Then I went and got dressed. I met Mark at the front door. He was getting his socks on. I had my socks on. I had my coat on. I pulled my shoes on. Opened the door. Looked out. It was snowing. This was the third day of snow. Mark said, Don't open the door yet. So I closed it. He finished tying his shoes. Pulled on his coat. We went outside. I turned, locked the door.

Went down to the garage. Pulled the car out. Mark went to get
in the car. I gestured to him. Close the garage, I mouthed. He
turned. Went to the garage. Closed the door. He got in the car.
Said, I don't know where my head is these days.

21. Chip a poem onto a stone tablet and give it to the world. Listen quietly. Watch rain to find an opening. Find someplace to enter passion. Fill the empty intonation of the falling with substance. It is early. The heart keeps her here when she seems so restless to go. Look wounded. Run through the river. Face drenched in night. And when you put your poem on paper, the falling is lost. Why do I hunger so? You practice for death.

Listen. She clears her throat. Look at her messed up hair. God I love her. I wish she would go back over the hill and stay there. I love her best from afar. Or in a picture. Or when she calls me on the phone. She can't think of what to say when she calls me on the phone. There's this long silence when she calls me on the phone. That's when she really knocks my socks off. When she calls me up on the phone and there is that long silence.

I lose track of what everybody calls me. For long periods of my life, I thought you had to see the bible to understand, bring it onto your own little horizon, so to speak. Just before I go upstairs I save the document I'm working on.

Hearts can be mended, he said. I need a new one of those black candy dispensers. Morton walked through the entire performance yesterday. The shoes came down harder on the hardwood floors. The carpet got stained. The windows were opaque. Thirty times was too many. Did you ever see one of those books where they put a picture of a skull in? It might be a medical book. Or a reference text. Do you ever wonder, when you look at one of those books, Whose skull is that? They don't say whose skull it is. There's nothing in the caption about whose skull it is. They probably don't even know whose skull it is. They just found it on the ground somewhere and for some reason they put it in a book. But that skull was somebody's head once.

Once upon a time, my mother saw me and I was there. I was born. What is a CFO? Mother whispered. She didn't want anyone to hear her. But there was no one there. Just the light from the window on the left side of her face. Dark shadows in the corners. Everyone gone. The house silent. More bossy men heroes came over the hill. They were on their way to the store. They needed milk. Cold cuts. Bronze items.

Sylvan was so cute. He looked like Frankenstein a little, only less square of a head, and no bolts on his neck. Mother didn't want anyone to hear her. Under her dress, things sat like they always had. Preserves stood in jars on shelves beneath the living room floor. Jam. Pickles. Beets. I fell asleep on the couch. The sun crossed over the house and touched my cheek through the window. The cat licked its paw in the corner. The fireplace was dark. All I wanted was to sleep. I opened my eyes. Hi cat. Hi man. Can you tell me who is Lois? I had not heard of Lois. I felt bad to disappoint the cat. I'm not evil. Just fat. Hoofs? Yes, those are hoofs.

I got the squeeze. But I could still see out the window. I could also see Aldo. And his brother. Clem. Those fuckers. Hair the colour of straw. It stuck up like straw, too. This was a windy place. The boys stood in the wind. Their hair went back, bounced forward. They bounded around the yard like happy bounding dogs. In the barn, the horses blew steam. Stamped. Made that horse noise they make with their lips.

It was midnight. Someone had died down the block. We didn't know who. Mother had already gone home. We didn't know it at the time, but we would never see her again.

We have also been making a group playground! You have to do a problem and a solution. Our problem was that the mayor wouldn't make a playground and we needed one! Our solution: a dragon came and burned down city hall! A playground fell out of the dragon's wings. We were happy.

Turn and start to run. But it hurts almost immediately. Without thinking, heal the break. The pain lingers as a memory. Keep leaping through the underbrush. I should be less noisy, he thought. But he kept crashing. Whoever, or whatever it was that was following him, continued in pursuit. He could hear something in pursuit. He turned. He needed to get somewhere he could camp for a few days. He needed to find food. He continued to wonder, What would want to chase after me? It must be the boy, he thought. He was torn by his desire to see the boy and his knowledge that such a meeting would not be prudent.

He come down from Ojibwa country, the old man bellered. A jar of mustard and a bag of pickles in his pack. It was a kind of song, only he didn't sing it. Have you ever looked at words and seen how they fall, one after another, but then not been able to figure out how all this falling culminates in what it culminates in?

22. I don't ever know what love looks like until you come back and give it to me again and then I find out again that it's more than I knew before. When I get there, I'm alone at the edge of the sea, looking out. I look back along the beach, along the path leading away from the beach into the trees. I look for you. I look for someone to show this to. The pink sky fanning over the water, which rumbles quietly, pitching itself about. But there's no one here. I'm alone, far ahead of anything I've ever known before and no one behind me to hold onto me and make me unafraid.

I looked at the trees one day when I was still a youth. My friend, said the tree closest to me. But then, it said, I engage a radically different concept of friendship from yours. A concept that sits at the endmost edge of a shimmering green leaf, high on a tall tree, in the wind, like a speck of dust clinging gently, momentarily, before being swept away with the general storm of dust that flees past us every day.

The boy allowed the ship to bob silently on the water for

many days before even contemplating a landing. During these days, he remained mostly in his cabin, looking out the porthole.

Ella roamed deep into the craw of a multi-layered morning – sun slanting, trees shadowed, field whispering. God, Ella felt, should be here to see this. This is God, Ella whispered. And what is cannot see itself as it is. For it continually continues to become. God was a becoming and Ella was part of that becoming. She wanted to fall into God like a drop of rain falls into a river caught up suddenly in an unrelenting current, thrust forward, then suddenly calm, lapping out into an ocean, where what lies beneath grows ever deeper. Ella felt herself more and more just a surface; a flat, fleshy moment, drifting gently over the void.

The sun is coming up, Dad. I can see cars on the highway. I think you might have told me once that I could phone you anytime. I'm by the window here. You're dead, so I can't phone you now. The sun is touching many things in my apartment, giving them new meaning, new life, new ways of touching my eyes. I have coffee. Steam rises off the cup.

Is capturing a metaphoric silence in words friendlier than an actual silence? When is it time to stop writing? What new beginning is impossible to accomplish until writing ends?

I wanted you to take me away from there. But you opened the door so I could go back into my life. And I cried.

The world as all encompassing, unfathomable existence sets no rules for proceeding. You want to experience full acceptance, but such acceptance is to feel God's essential, absolute, unbroachable indifference. To see the pickup truck travel across the bridge there on the other side of the parking lot, while the sun comes up and stains the few streaks of cloud in the west pink, is to understand how things slow down and then, finally, stop and hover and wait.

I was in the shower again, thinking about the effect of what my sister-in-law said. What my sister-in-law said was about the difference between toast and Eggo waffles. This baffled me. I considered everything. I considered what the weather had been the day she spoke to me. I considered what I saw out the glass patio doors behind my sister-in-law. I considered what I saw of the day, and the trees that sat beneath the day, like revolutions with roots. I saw everything but Eggo waffles.

Any reading of *Lord of the Rings* should be done within an hour after you get out of the shower. As well you know, Tolkien was completely in earnest. Absolutely sincere. A true believer. It doesn't matter what he believed. Just that he believed. Whatever it was he believed, he believed in it wholly, with all his spirit. Such belief, such entirely unquestioning belief, must be witnessed with clean hair.

The Johanson twins jogged by outside the front window. They were wearing matching yellow jackets. We could see out the front window to the street and the sidewalk and the houses across the road. The Johanson twins had jackets that were mustard yellow. Within seconds of us seeing them outside the window on the sidewalk, the Johanson twins were gone. I went out the front door to get the paper. My bath steamed. Glancing through the paper, I could see no sign of the Johanson twins. Later in the day, it snowed like a real blizzard. Nothing you were quite expecting, but there it was. Mike Pollit walked by with his dog, Arf. Mike was bundled up. Hat, scarf, gloves, puffy coat. But it was Mike's dog who looked cold. Mike still had the close cropped beard. He was wearing sunglasses. Sam had never heard anyone play the drums like Mike Pollit.

Sometimes, at night, when he looks up at the stars, Mark

hears a voice asking him, Which dimension would you rather inhabit, Mark? Mark waits. What are my choices? he wonders, with respect to dimensions? But the voice says no more. Mark goes back in to kiss pregnant Lily goodnight. But she is already asleep. On her back. A tiny mountain under the bed covers. He hates to wake her. How long was he outside looking at stars? Waiting for the voice to return? How long was I there? he asks himself. No one wants answers, he answers. Mark feels alone.

My wife sat at the foot of the bed with her bathrobe open. The hill rose. Pretty soon, men came over the crest, the red sun behind them, their black silhouettes crossing and re-crossing indiscriminately, threatening the great universal intravascular system with their intrusive chaos.

That guy really likes to sit by his desk and look at the stuff he has on it. He has a cup of coffee. He has papers. Books. A couple of staplers. Some tape dispensers. CD cases. A vase with nothing in it. He lays on his back on the floor. There is a knife on the desk. He can hear the kids talking to the woman in the kitchen. That library had no upstairs, says the girl. Yes it did, says the boy. But the woman says nothing. There is a briefcase beside the desk with a red decal stuck on it.

People were shopping. They looked nice. Happy. The girl with the white hat was looking at pillows with sparkly dogs on them. She looked at cushioned, cone-shaped containers with Santa ornaments in them. Sand castles. Some women laughed. The older woman moved slowly. The man looked stunning. Stunned. Starry-eyed. I'm coming home, he thought. If I go on a trip, it will be like shopping for two weeks.

It hurt for the first five minutes. But this was permanent. Your head is different. My head's not different. The setting sun lit the clouds hovering over the horizon like a dream beyond

the grasping fingers of weed trees rising up on the vacant lot
behind the Rapid Lube. My face is older. My hairline is receding.
But my head is the same as it always was. People's heads don't
change. Some people's heads are like tall foundation blocks,
with dark fields of close-cropped grass, at right angles to each
other. Some people's heads seem to run in fear from their eyes.

Bicycles locked to steel guy wires propping up tall wooden
light poles. Light poles start out straight, but, over the years,
they tilt.

Are you awake? Yes. Can you sleep? I can. Why aren't you
then? I don't want to. Do you want to talk? No. Is there such a
word as interiority? No. There should be. Why? Just because
you think a word that isn't a word should be a word, you think
it should actually be a word? It would be a useful word; people
would use it. What people? People like you? Let me tell you,
buster, you're one of a kind. You'd be the only one using a stupid
word like that. Like what? Like that stupid word you think
should be a real word. And what word is that, Drew? I don't
know, that stupid word you made up. If you don't even know
what word it is, how do you know it's a stupid word?

Tiny had nothing but her decision to stay. It floated in the
air around her like a ribbon of wind, whirling by her face
maddeningly. It dipped beneath her knees, so that she had to
twirl and jump and swing her head about to keep it in view. It
was bright and silver, but indistinct, hazy, impossible to get into
focus. It dodged into the wood like a tiny metal bird looking
for a roost. Then slunk across the grass like a snake. Tiny tried
to step on it. She jumped about wildly. The sky grew dark. The
moon peeked over trees.

My mother came over and sat on the porch for a while. When
she left, I closed the porch door and looked out the window.

I turned on the porch light. Moths flew up. After a while I went to bed. I could hear things going on outside. Planes flew over. Cars drove by. Once in a while, I'd hear voices. Some of the voices were women, some were men. They all sounded happy. That made me feel afraid. There were people who thought they could do things. Mrs. Harrison thought she could write book reviews. Mr. Palmateer thought he could sing. You could hear him in his living room at night, singing with a scratchy record going in the background. When I went to bed at night, I pulled the covers up around my neck and turned out the light. For a long time I couldn't see anything. Then, after a while, I could see the outlines of things. I'd start remembering things for no reason. Like the week we took Sammy camping at Sauble Falls. He was three. There was a kid his age on a nearby campsite. The father chopped wood and drove around the campground in a pickup truck. We took Sammy to the beach every day. But Sammy hated the beach.

23. I was to go out on the weekends. I was to take no one with me. I was to look for shoes. I opened the screen door as silently as I could. The air hit me like water bumping up against the base of a cliff. Everyone in the neighbourhood was gone. Sammy's friends were gone. They leave their lights on when they go. They get in their cars. They go. They go in every direction. Sometimes you'll hear a plane. Otherwise, everything is quiet. I go in the kitchen. Feed Tommy. I give him rice and blue Gatorade. When the sickness lifts, I feel light. Sammy hardly ever comes upstairs anymore. He'll soon be six.

Easter came. Then Star Trek came.

He puts me in a file cabinet. He takes the file cabinet to the trunk of his car. Puts it in. He backs his car into a driveway. Knocks on the file cabinet. You okay in there, he says. He gets the file cabinet out of the trunk. Takes it through a door. Carries the file cabinet downstairs. He puts the file cabinet in a corner. He shows me how to work the doors. I give him some orange juice. I give him a tea biscuit. He sits in the file cabinet with me for a bit. Eats his tea biscuit. Drinks his orange juice. He gets up. As if to leave. He stands by the file cabinet. Taps his fingers on the top of it. Shakes his head. Goes out the front door.

I bring a book up to bed with me. Tutti says, Don't you want to talk to me? I get out of bed. Go along the hall. There's no light except the light coming from the little night light in the bathroom. Shining faintly on the wood floor. I go into the office. Close the door. I put on the light in the office. I lean back against the closed door. I go across the office. Stop at my bookshelf. Pull out a book. I fall asleep with my head on the desk. Later in the night, I go downstairs. Pee. I go in the kitchen. Pour a glass of orange juice. Drink. I stand in the light from the open fridge. I pour another glass of orange juice. Put the orange juice container back in the fridge. Close the fridge. Stand in the dark, by the sink, drinking orange juice.

I have a creeping suspicion it is a hot wind, says Mom. She has fingered the blinds open a crack. She's looking out. I go out to the car. This is a hot wind, I think. I go over to the grocery store. It's six-thirty. The grocery store is out of corn and watermelon. I buy rice and eggs. When I hit the bird with the car, I am travelling south on Castle Rock Drive. I am daydreaming. In the daydream, Sammy is sixteen and I am being nice to him and he loves me as much as he did when he was four.

Tom looks so normal. But he's not. He's insane. He's actually insane. Although they've yet to lock him up. But they will. They might lock him up. One day. If they can see beyond the photo. See the way he turns sideways to smile at you beautifully. He's obviously less than beautiful. But the photo prohibits something. Something his words never conceal. If you could see him moving, you would see. You would see he moves in strange ways. Sloshing. Like he's sloshing against mud that he feels is up to his chin. Mud that threatens always to rise up and fill his mouth. He has to smile so hard to keep from showing fear. He's frantic. He loves Vienna Teng. And not in a healthy way.

The earliest things those guys used to do at the mall was dig up the flowers by the entrance and plant them in front of somebody's house. They had a piano.

They should do the procedure, I thought. But then it turned out they couldn't do the procedure. I thought, The guy is fucked. He's fucked. But what should you expect in the fifth year? He's the most beautiful creature you could ever imagine. More so, of course, because he's nude. Which means you could never imagine. So don't even try. He stood by the wall across from the showers. He looks very small in my mind when I try to picture this. He looks small and lost. He wasn't quite six. He was standing in his bathing suit while I showered. I turned my face up to wash the chlorine off my face. When I looked back, he was gone.

I went to see. To have seen the procedure was a much desired state of being. To have produced the supposed stick inside the city. This would prevent the procedure from being anything more than what people said it was.

I bought a magazine. I don't think anyone wanted to read, though. They kept talking about George Stone.

Scientists can say this sort of thing: First, and most tragically, this means everything we can know is an idiot's dream that may or may not be best suited to the objectivity one objectifies nonetheless.

I, Ken Sparling, am an object. You may or may not know that I remain to be seen. But it is only a matter of time.

We are called upon to hold things together. Our relationships unethical. Our relationships are the entire cultural tradition of

24. The writer isn't actually dead, of course. The death is a metaphoric, language-based death, which we know since birth. It is a death of which we often speak.

Mary locked the door of the library, then stood on the stoop, her hand on the doorknob, unwilling to turn and face the evening that waited behind her. She could see an ephemeral reflection of herself in the darkened glass of the door she'd just locked. Within and beyond this reflection, she could see the edge of the circulation desk on the right and three of the paperback spinners on the left. And she could see through to the front window of the library, just a narrow segment of it, but enough to see a small child, his face pressed to the window, hand above his forehead to block out the light and better see into the library.

They say the writer is dead. But they say he is dead only in a metaphoric sense. The writer is lost to the reader. The words on the page contain the writer's lament at being lost to the reader, for the reader does not experience the loss as a loss of writer, but as a recovering of what was forgotten. For the reader, the writer constitutes an absolute absence, at least to the extent that the writing is successful in resurrecting a memory. But what gets remembered?

For a moment, Mary considered going back into the library, unlocking the front door and finding out what the child was hoping for. What was the child hoping for? But, she decided, she would not be able to get back into the library, disarm the alarm, and get to the front door before the boy was gone. Perhaps, Mary thought, the child is hoping that his experience of the object as a plurality of moments was coming to an end. Maybe his ability to go on living depends on him understanding the singularity of an object, even in the face of evidence to the contrary. Don't move, Mary told the boy, but she was in the heart of the flame, rising deep into the lie of drama. If every object became anew with every shift of the head, the boy would surely go mad. Yet, Mary, is it not still possible for us to encounter the object anew? Is the stabilizing of the object world, lie that it is, not a very necessary lie?

If the loss remains metaphoric, if the writer does not truly allow for his death in the writing, then he will find himself starting his story this way: You can only ever hope that the weather will improve, commented Hoover to his wife. Is your name really Hoover, Wendy asked. Is your name really Wendy? No one can tell us for sure. Go ahead and try. Try to find out. You can't find out. You can't.

If we were both dreaming, me of you, you of me, and we reached out toward each other...But we wouldn't be able to breathe. Wouldn't be able to breathe? No. I don't understand. When you reach out of a dream, it's like being underwater. You can't breathe.

Mary returned the boy's gaze for a moment, then looked at her hands. Can you tell me a story? the boy asked. Mary looked up. The boy was still staring, unblinking, into her eyes. Mary felt a welter of panic rise from her stomach to her chest. Then it entered her throat and threatened to choke her.

Moonlight Sonata has been one of the most exciting pieces for me to learn, because it has caused me to rework the fingering so many times and I'm still not sure which fingering is the best in a couple cases. I have to try to see ahead to where I get more fluent and try to speculate which fingering is worth investigating more fully. I initially stumbled across sheet music for a shortened version of the piece for violin and piano and typed it into Guitar Pro so I could print out a banjo tab. I knew that the Béla version was a lot longer, but I thought I could learn the beginning this way. There was one place in the piece where I had to go from the first string/seventeenth fret to the fourth string/first fret. I kept working at it, and sometimes I made it sound okay, but it seemed impossible to make it reliably smooth. Then, when I went to learn the rest of the Béla version by putting Perpetual Motion on the slow downer, I realized Béla was playing a half-tone lower and therefore going from the sixteenth fret/first string to an open fourth string! Cool. But then I had to relearn the piece a fret down. I had been tuning the fifth string to G$^\sharp$ to get an open string G$^\sharp$ which helped with some of the transitions and I realized now that I could just do it in standard G tuning.

He was high up on a cliff, overlooking the ocean, and each change in the ocean, each crashing wave, each little dove of spray that flew up and dissipated, made his eyes narrow in thought. All the things that might have happened, that might still happen. He raised his eyebrows, his lips parted, he looked like a happy baby, safe and happy and naïve. Children are made of marble, he thought. He watched the spray fly up like it would attack him, but it fell far short each time, retreating back to the sea like some angry monster that couldn't catch its breath.

Here? Mary asked, trying to keep the panic from her voice. She held her head steady and forced herself to look the boy in the face. Were his lips blue? she wondered. It might just be the light. Mary didn't think he looked cold. He wasn't shivering. He looked calm. His eyes were quiet. He said nothing. I can't tell you a story here, Mary said. I don't have a book. She'd never told a story straight out of her head. I suppose I could if I tried, she thought. But, in truth, the idea terrified her. Shreds of smoky cloud whispered across the space of sky that was visible between the buildings that rose above Mary and the boy, like ghosts crossing a highway. All of a sudden it was growing dark, but the sky still held enough light to lend it a blue luminescence that seemed disconcertingly out of place in the darkening city as Mary stood waiting for the boy to speak. Mary's breath was visible in the frigid air, drifting and morphing like the clouds above them. The boy's breath rose gently to join Mary's in the air between them. The boy looked toward the library entrance, up the street from where they stood. Mary looked in the same direction. She understood that the boy wanted her to take him into the library. I don't live in the library, she said, laughing a little. She looked at the boy and caught a moment of panic in his eyes and her own panic melted away. She let out a long slow breath and felt the muscles in her shoulders and neck slacken. She suddenly saw the boy's vulnerability and her heart took over and reached out.

If you looked as far as you could to the north. Yes? That's it. That's it? Yes. You've got to give me more. That's all I know.

This is disorienting; what can this possibly tell me? It starts off with if. It's a good sentence. There's something good in it. It somehow feels complete. I don't get it. If sets up a limitless void of possibility fixed into irrevocable staticisity. Jesus, that's a good sentence, too. I know, but wait, because you throws responsibility for the motionlessness of if away from the speaker, detaching him, making him an ineffectual spectator. You expands the limitlessness of the void If by tearing it from its narrative root, setting it adrift.

Winter. The sun is shining, but there's no heat. My feet are frozen. I'm out in the driveway in my slippers. I look up. One cloud, not moving, puffy white, the sky behind it washed out, almost white. Evergreens. Snow. To write is to deny myself access to the place I am trying to go. So why do I write?

I'm learning to play Beethovan's Moonlight Sonata on the banjo. At one point, Beethovan imagined moving from a simple three note major chord arpeggio to another fairly simply three note arpeggio, but I think on a minor chord this time, a third up from the major chord. It's a sweet little transition on the banjo. The middle finger of the fretting hand slides up one fret, the hand pivoting around that middle finger, the ring finger dropping from the fourth to the first string and the index finger moving up from the second string to the fourth. It looks deceptively simple. I mean, to me, it looks deceptively simple. It even feels deceptively simple. The first time I realized how it worked, I thought, great. Because there are places in the piece where the transitions are difficult. I mean, just getting my fingers from one place to the next is a challenge, let alone making it sound clean and smooth and anything approximately the sound of beauty Beethovan must have had in mind. But this transition from the major to the minor arpeggio is easy in terms of moving my fingers. Somehow, though, it's turned out to be one of the most dreaded transitions I make in the piece, because my ring finger almost invariably causes the open fourth string to sound when I try to move it to the first string. I've tried using the heel of my picking hand to dampen the fourth string and stop it sounding. I've tried lifting my ring finger off the fourth string very carefully, straight up. Either of these methods works sometimes. But not always and I have to work very consciously to make them happen. Somehow I resent this having to pay so much attention, especially to a move I've made so many times. Partly, I think, it's because I expected it to be so easy. That was my mistake I think, expecting it to be easy.

The writer, in the act of writing, is reanimating himself in his concession to the absence of animation. The writer experiences an awakening from the sensuous accompaniment of death in the act of writing. This is what makes the writer suffer. But what is this compulsion to write if it draws the writer out of his one project – to die?

The compulsion to write lies on the horizon, that place out ahead, whatever the particularities of that place might be. It is the seemingly hopeless, yet equally unavoidable compulsion to take a step, the next step, but the compulsion is not in the character of the next step itself, for it would be easy enough to take a step in one or the other direction. No, the compulsion lies in the hope of grounding that step, of gaining ground, of moving in on the horizon, which is, let us be reminded, always simply death. We are to take seriously the horizon. Give it its due. We are to understand the horizon as something beyond the line of a beautiful sunset or the silhouette of a city as we approach from afar. The setting of the sun is certainly the end of something. We are asking: how is the loss of the end of the day going to help us with our project, which, remember, is to die.

It was raining and I took Oosker to the magazine store. I wanted to get the magazines and see what they were saying, so I took Oosker out of the house and put him in the car. When we got to the plaza where the magazine store is, I got Oosker out of the car and put him on the sidewalk. He kept stepping off the sidewalk into the road. I kept picking him up and putting him back on the sidewalk. Stay on the sidewalk, I told him. Finally I picked him up and carried him into the magazine store. You can go into those places. Those stores, I mean. You can go right into them. You don't have to knock. You can just walk right in. I told Oosker this as we were going into the store. I put my lips to his ear and you could see in his eyes that he was listening. You can just go right in, I whispered. And then I looked in his eyes to see if he was listening. It's like meeting someone you don't even know when you look into Oosker's eyes like that. It's like no one could ever belong to anyone, like Oosker is out in the middle of a field of snow, alone in the middle and you can't get onto the field of snow. You can walk and walk and walk, but you'll never get onto it.

After they had been married a few years they went out and got hot dogs. Hot dogs were a thing they could touch. After work. In a pinch. At odd and often unexpectedly appropriate times.

Writing is a manner by which to discover meaning. Poetry seems most prepared for this. The act of discovering meaning seems central to the arrangement of words in poetry. Poetry seems prepared to discover meaning. It seems to come to the table unarmed with meaning. Poetry seems to come upon meaning as it moves across the page. Editing your words is an act of savagery. You are thrown upon your words. Your words lost among each other. Lost to you. So. Not your words. Not now, as you revisit. The savageness of the impulse is what must be met and resisted. Resisted precisely in the meeting. Resistance becomes a kind of holding onto. A shaking of other. Your words now reencountered. The savagery of the edit is what will ring in the reader's mind.

So, one day, I won't be at this desk. One day, my life will change, and stretch on like something perfect, like a perfect walk in a perfect forest, with dew dripping off the trees and the forest floor spongy under my feet. I will see bears and I will run and dive into rivers.

If I were a tree, I'd live on one of those hills in the Lake District in England, where the trees, from a distance, look like green carpets. From a distance, you cannot notice the gentle movement of the individual branches. There are horses on the edge of the fields and the fields roll and then end, like they were the end of everything.

I've read entire books from their beginnings to their ends. I've read them from their beginnings, where their first words are on the page. Their first words telling me the first things they are there to say and it's only the first words I have, the first words and then a deep grey silence, a huge sea of grey silence.

25. When she goes out of sight of the peephole, I'm tempted to open the door. Look out. I don't hear Tish moving around in bed so I go back into the bedroom. I stand in the doorway.

There was a stereo hooked up to an intercom system that broadcast to some distant planet. Each room in the house was a record turned on by a volume knob. The volume knob was analog. I could see people at the windows. Fans of mine. Looking in. Yelling. But I couldn't hear their stories. Only their mouths opening. Opening. Opening.

When she danced, she had to put her foot down, and when she put her foot down, she had to touch the earth.

I better go talk to that guy again, John said. They can't do this. This was not the agreed upon arrangement. John stood. He was a tall man, accustomed to stooping. Slim. With lines on his face. That year was the longest of any of them, but no colder. I put the ladder on the wall and set one foot on the bottom rung.

I rode to a workplace one particular scratchy day. Snatches of a story riding into my head. The unthinkable being thought.

Lapses within the pool of momentary memory were giving me remarkable power. I was definitive proof of man's infinite capacity. I didn't get the job. We'll have to lie to the kids about that. One day we'll be on the couch. We'll remember our lies. Like music fading to a memory. But before that happens, we'll realize that reading is lonely, because, no matter how skillfully we do it, we are each of us alone at the end.

Stella looks as though she can't be bothered. As though she'd be wasting her breath. You should get your own fucking notebook, she says. But she says it like she's never heard anyone talk before. Like language is something new to her. It is winter. It is cold. Every paragraph she speaks seems destined to deteriorate into a rain of meaning. When a sentence works, it is like the music of knowing the hum that follows her through her life. As she teeters on the edge of oblivion, she remembers seeing the back of a woman in mist. At that moment, she knows that the woman she saw that night in the mist was the woman she loved.

Going at the same speed you are going at brings you to the knowledge that even if the speed you are going is really fast, it becomes less and less apparent how fast you are actually going until after you find yourself alone, going slow, making crappy little jerky movements, impressing no one. Streets that went straight get eaten in swirls of curling dust. The silence is really a noise. The silence is actually a low hum. A hum you didn't hear for years. Then, when you finally heard it, you realized it was there all along. You need a piece of jewellery with emeralds and pearls. You need to wear it on Thursday. This will heal you.

A woman comes home from work. She passes a man on the front porch. Dark heavy clouds have been hovering over the house for days. The shadows of clouds drift across the ground.

They make everything on earth look dark. Sometimes, but mainly not, rain falls. But mainly just clouds drift rainless on a windswept sky. The woman goes into the house. After a while, she comes back out. She has puffy eyes. What are you sleeping on at night? she asks the man. Clouds, the man says.

A silent tractor rode the horizon as though it were riding a road. Stephen put his hands together. Prayed. God wasn't even there. There was a guy who looked like God. The guy had glasses. Maybe God got glasses, I thought. The guy was all the way at the other end of the pool. That's not God, I thought. I didn't say anything to Stephen. Let him pray, I thought.

He is standing on a beehive. The beehive is under a rock in the driveway. He is tall. He thought it was because there were shortages. You can make them out of glass, she told him. They were standing together at the end of the driveway. Each had their own power. Each of them had a certain power that it was good for them to pass along to each other.

The woman goes to a house to get her palms read. Psychic, it says on the lawn. The psychic gives the woman a computer printout. The woman keeps the printout in a manila envelope on her desk. She never goes to the psychiatrist. When it is almost time to start work, she opens the envelope. Gets the printout. She pulls it out of the manila envelope. She doesn't understand the lines on the printout. The lines on the printout look like blue mountains. The psychic believes in a world below blue mountains.

Some grand overall purpose has been embraced. I look for days at defeat. The sort of defeat that allows you to characterize the space inside dust. I place two words next to each other with no regard for their individual well-being. It took four days to understand this fully.

She knew something. She was diving. I know, she said. She was alone in a car. She was talking to the windshield. Her smile grew out of something inside, like a parasite growing vine-like from her tonsils.

It seemed that they'd made a perfect chance for themselves. Try as they might, though, they could not see each other. Most of the time they did not even try to see what was happening in life all around them, the way you wouldn't happen to see your cat in the morning if you stayed on the rug being perfectly quiet.

Nice plan, she thought.

It's a nice place, this financial institution, Mary said. They were talking on the phone. Matty in the country. Her friend in the city. You can get some real good soup at the scriptorium, Mary said. That, in itself, can bring some satisfaction. She had no fucking idea what she was talking about. How God plays with us, she thought. Good as He is. She couldn't tell. One moment, the next car is coming over the hill; the next moment, all that's left is the silence that follows rubber rolling frantically on pavement. He could have been driving any car. Maybe something green. Write the same word over and over again. If it makes you afraid, think how very good it is that you haven't had much practice. Spend a lot of time writing the same word. The part of the sentence that you gauge to be the middle seems good. To myself, I think, good God, what have you become? But to others, that middle part might look very good indeed.

What is it, Doc? I asked. Nothing to worry about, the doctor told me. We'll run some tests. But rain will come in the night. Next day, dark clouds will spread thick above the city, like butter on a pancake. Each man, as he gazes about himself, will inhabit only a small moment. City streets will spread, rush forth, turn, burst back. Gentle declamations unto themselves.

Something made him laugh. Why do we know with such certainty when the phone is taken away from the ear? Everything will be yellow, he said. The boy will sit. We will sip our drinks. We will not look at each other. The boy will lean back against the trunk of the tree and look out into the heat shimmering over the fields. The shimmering heat will be yellow. The cool liquid in our glasses will be yellow also.

When a person phones and wants to tell another person she loves him, is that how we know who the people are who are phoning us?

They go out to the car. They go to the bank. They stop at the mall. They come home with parcels. They walk up the walk. They live in a house. A little house with a walk that goes from the driveway to the front door.

26. When she came to town she felt popular. She was there to see her sister. But she was there to see a man, too. She stood in front of a mirror. She was in her sister's bedroom. Her sister was at work. She was imagining how this man would see her. What he would see when he saw her. She had makeup on. Her eyes were beautiful. She knew this for a fact. A door opened and she tumbled through. He leapt toward her. She could feel her heart beat. She had on a flower-print dress. Cream coloured. With yellow and blue flowers. And something orange she could see from the corner of her eye. She wanted toast. She wanted coffee. She had quit smoking recently, but she wanted a cigarette. She was hungry. What could fill this emptiness? The capital was Belwok. The carpet felt soft under her bare feet. If she could, she would have gone to meet the man in bare feet. The man lived in Belwok. Her legs were solid. The skin on her calves and shins was firm. Her legs emerged from her dress. They emerged just above her knees. She looked down. Tried to see her knees. The dress belled. It blocked her view. She couldn't see her knees.

There were hours between herself by the mirror and herself by the man. She had no idea what was coming. What she thought this day would bring was not at all what it would bring. She left the mirror. Went to the window. Parted the curtains. Peered out. There was a bit of light now. In the east. A deep blue at the edge of the sky. But she could still see stars. She smiled to herself. It would be a good day. She removed her dress. She laid it carefully over the back of a chair. She eased the straps of her slip off her shoulders. She went back to the mirror. She wanted to see what the man would see. She thought what she saw was what others saw. What the man saw. What the man saw every day from the moment he opened his eyes in the morning to the moment he closed them again in bed at night. What the man saw deep inside the night on nights when he lay awake. This seeing that brought him what he saw was not what others saw. What the woman saw now in the mirror was a thickness. Her shoulders truly pleased her. Soft, they seemed. She shifted her body. She sought a flattering angle. The skin on her shoulders shimmered with light. They shimmered as though light emanated from the woman's skin. From somewhere inside, the woman felt something quicken. She glanced about quickly. She thought she might find her soul pulsating in the light she shed. She felt in this light a sense of the infinite. Whereas the man saw only the tops of things. Suggestions jutting out of buildings. Jutting out of sidewalks. Out of trees. Out of squirrels. People. Tables. Coat racks. Hats, grass, flies. Things seemed to poke toward the man's life, then pull away. They pulled away so quickly, he could never see what lay beneath the tip of anything. The woman felt thickest in the middle. She felt a thickness she couldn't shed. The thickness seemed deliberate. She'd been afraid of that thickness since forever. She reached behind and up her back.

27. Clive was feeling a jog coming on. Salivating. He felt longing from having been swimming in the pool. So close to a single blonde hair caught in the pool filter. He loved the baby. Just like everybody else. But. In a way, it made him sad. It had been nice feeling sad. Sitting on the sidewalk in the rain. Even having a dad who was becoming a Republican felt nice and sad. Oh, Clive, Clive, Clive. Come. Learn to love the dad. He's been nice to the brothers. Felt. Terry cloth. A bit of a warm smile inside.

Time to move on, he said gently. Lie in your bed at night. See if you fall asleep. Make a list. In your head. List the nights. Another terrible headache coming. He hadn't told anyone. He dreamed for the feeling of riding.

The sun shone through the window over the sink. David sat in the breakfast nook, sideways to the window. The sun hit his cheek. He could smell bacon and eggs and toast and coffee. He could smell cigarette smoke coming in. Through the kitchen window. He'd seen the pictures. Blackened lungs. Fear made you pee yourself, or come in your pants. Anger was a way to

224

stop fear. A kind of control. One day, David thought, I opted for
control. Another day, I opted to control the anger. Like a double
negative, David's double control blackened his heart.

Every night he wanted me to read to him. I want a story, he
said. Okay, I said. This is the story of...but he stopped me. Not
that story, he said. Okay, I said. Cook something, he said. When
you cook something, you become quiet. She seemed sad. But she
was only caught in the web of her salad dressing. She crushed a
clove of garlic in her garlic press. She scraped the garlic off the
press with a knife. She turned on the cold water tap. Flushed
the pulp from the garlic press into the sink. The pulp swirled in
water. Settled in the small basket in the drain. She put the garlic
press in the sink. She cut the top off the flower of garlic with
the single clove missing. She poured olive oil over the garlic.
Wrapped the garlic in foil wrap. Put the foil wrapped garlic in
the oven. On the top shelf. She put the oven on broil. What is
this? she asked herself. She went to the cupboard by the cat dish.
Her feet were bare. They hung from her ankles like creatures
with independent existences.

Is there anything that looks like prose? Mary wonders. She
looks out her window, hoping for baby ducks. Tiny baby ducks
lined up behind their mother. Or pigeons strung out on hydro
lines. There is nothing else, she decides. No one remembers
prose. Anything I could squish together and make it look like
prose wouldn't even cover the grass. The grass isn't even totally
covered. And the man in the hat, waiting across the street, has
already waited through three green lights.

You do a little curtsy and a grin. Suddenly, I have agreed to
these vague memories. I have agreed to these diversions, these
diverse relations of yours. These people on farms. I endeavour
to imagine what I've always remembered. Your grandparents,

living in Selkirk. People in places I imagined were a long drive in no particular direction. I think of that place as Selkirk.

I was driving to work. The rain had stopped. But it was totally cloudy. I was sitting in the car, not moving, stuck in traffic. Waiting. There was a cabbage on the side of the road. I wrote in my day timer: phone yourself. Do it today. Remind yourself in an e-mail. It isn't too late. Do it now. But I couldn't remember what it was exactly that I wanted to remind myself to do. I decided that I really only wanted to remind myself of something, and what I reminded myself of was nothing.

I wound up being Ken all my life. I didn't expect that. I thought at some point I would be someone else.

EPILOGUE Me? I'm off to the office again. But nothing was ever for sure. Nothing ever came of what I expected. Everything could come from what was needed to come. I got a second season of love. They were offering those large green books for free again. They never foresaw the demand. After I got the green book, I pissed everything away. The money. The Tupperware containing voices. All the leaves gone. Sucked into a vortex. The second season of Star Trek came at Easter. The short one got me into the living room. Turned off the lights. Held me down.